TALL WAR

TALL WAR

THE STARBUCK WARS
VOLUME 1

STEPHEN HOUSER
award winning author

A Novel by Stephen Houser
Copyright © 2022 by Stephen Houser
Lionel A Blanchard, Publisher

All rights reserved. No part of this publication may be reproduced, stored in a retrieval system, or transmitted, in any form or by any means, electronic, mechanical, photocopying, recording, or otherwise, without the prior written permission of the author.

This is a work of fiction. Names, characters, places, and incidents either are the product of the author's imagination or are used fictitiously.

Any resemblance to actual persons, living or dead, events, or locales is entirely coincidental.

First Printing

ISBN: 979-8-88796-264-1

Cover Art and Design by Vincent Chong

> We know nothing about them.
> Their language, their history,
> or what they look like.
> But we can assume this.
> They stand for everything
> we don't stand for.
>
> —Captain Zapp Branigan
>
> War is the H Word,
> Futurama

This book is dedicated to my charming and talented friend,
Dr. Gary D. Friedman.

CHAPTER 1

My wife is hot. Which is nice for me. She's also the president of the United States of America. Which is nice for her. For all that, Geness doesn't take herself too seriously. In fact, I think she enjoys the benefits of being hot just as much as she enjoys the benefits of being powerful.

When I say things like, "Bold leadership today, honey," or, "Way to handle the opposition, sweetheart," Geness blushes a little bit and smiles. But when I say, "That nightgown is blocking my agenda, Madam President. Why don't you just veto it?" all hell breaks loose. Lucky me.

Speaking of Gen, she's calling. I blink and bring my netacts lenses online. And voila, there she is. Red hair. Full lips. Emerald eyes.

"Come and see me, love," Gen purrs from somewhere deep in her throat.

"At work?" I ask surprised. Which, however, should not be confused with unwilling.

"Yes." Geness backs away from the desk cam, turns around, and yanks up her skirt, flashing me her pink, perfect behind. She watches me over her shoulder. "I just took a Viagrear," she says, then puckers and unpuckers her mouth to make sure I get it. I do.

"Don't get me hard in my RediMedi," I warn her standing up. "The last time you did that I got a safety soak from the suit and couldn't get it up again for twenty-four hours."

Geness drops her skirt and flips around. Her eyes are huge. Her beautiful face confused.

"I thought that wasn't supposed to happen unless you were erect for more than four hours," she says.

"Tell *that* to your mother. The suit was her birthday gift, remember?" At the time, I opened what looked like a top-of-the-line work suit and I was impressed. Corky, Gen's mom, is not my biggest fan. "She thought a PervPrevention suit would be a great gag," I go on, allowing myself to whine a little. "Too bad she didn't tell me that before I wore it."

"She was just trying to be funny, Ben," my wife says in her mother's defense. "I don't know how the heck she even got one of those. They're only issued to convicted sex offenders."

Well, everyone knows that. The suits are supposed to train predators to keep things under control by stripping them of any kind of sexual freedom. No urges, no issues. If the suit detects any erectile response, it instantly levels it with a ten percent alcohol soak.

"I was not entertained," I reply. "RediMedi wouldn't take it back and the most they would do was to tinker the existing suit down to a BehaviorSafe version."

"The one for high school kids?"

TALL WAR

"Yes."

"Well, at least *that* soak is just plain H2O," Gen responds, always mining the silver lining from life's small embarrassments. I have the opposite mindset. I am always very happy to point out whenever *anything* sucks.

"It was *ice cold* H2O," I remind my wife.

Geness grins and gives her hips a shake.

"Enough banter, lover boy," she says. "You've got to get all the way to the White House in the next ninety minutes."

I don't need to be told twice. My wife has a beautifully engineered body. Large breasts. Narrow hips. Bite-size ass. And no pubic or body hair anywhere. Except for her gorgeous red hair, which flows all the way down to her perfect outie. At six and one-half inches tall she towers over me. In fact, she's probably taller than just about anybody, anywhere, except for Beijingers, and their height has nothing to do with rice.

I am five inches and seven-sixteenths tall. I was designed for farm work. Designed with broad shoulders, strong pecs, and bigger than normal biceps. I have brown eyes and brown hair, which I wear a little bit long because Gen thinks it's sexy that way.

My name is Ben Katz. Actually, Benedict Katz. A strand of pope DNA was grafted into my helix to help me tolerate solitary work and some jerkoff genome architect thought it would be clever to stick me with a chunk of medieval pope. I can't remember if the DNA was from a French pope or an Italian one. Actually, I shouldn't bitch. The end result of that and the other socio-scientific manipulations of my architecture is that I am quite happy in my work as the solo operator of a small, state-owned dairy. And I'm not really alone at work. I have my cows.

I've been married to Gen for seven years. She was elected president on November 2, 2776, and has served almost nine months. She likes her new job. While I would never say it to her face, governing the republic is not quite the task it was for her predecessors. Today the United States is made up of Virginia, West Virginia, Maryland, Delaware, and the misshapen, never-fully-filled-in District of Columbia. We have a population of some twenty-six thousand citizens—mostly farmers—and my wife's main duty is to preside over Congress when it meets once a year in September to talk about how the cows and the crops did since the last time it met.

Members of Congress are volunteers and there are never very many. They bat about prices and export quotas for the upcoming year and then send their recommendations to the United Nations Food Authority. Their figures are reviewed and eventually passed on to the General Assembly, which controls planetary food production, prices, and distribution.

Our UN delegate is Rigging Nash, not incidentally the wealthiest and most conservative citizen we have. He was appointed by the Security Council and serves at its pleasure. Rigging wields the real power in our little nation. He lives full-time in New York City and votes every day on the UN issues brought before the all-powerful world government.

Blah, blah, blah. What does all this information mean? I don't really know. I just started thinking about this stuff this morning. Geness asked if I would spend some time each day remembering things about our lives so she can use it when she writes her Kindle about being president. I told her sure.

I mean, I'm busy with the cows and all, but she's not asking for a lot. I just think about whatever I want and my thoughts

TALL WAR

are transduced to digital code by my Thinking Cap. (Where do engineers come up with these names?) The cap is actually a membrane sheath filled with brain wave sensors. It conforms to the shape of my head with the same great look and feel of a latex condom.

Geness will use the data I record sooner or later, working it like pretzel dough into the shape she wants. Speaking of which, I told her that she shouldn't upload a final version of *anything* she writes to the cloud until she generates a printed product to protect her memoirs against the cyber slime who chew up new wikis. I know Wikipedia has always allowed this, but letting anyone who feels like it altar posted materials seems way out of line to me. And the more I think about it, the more determined I am to insist that Geness invest in a pulp-and-ink version of her memoirs. Hell, we can keep it at home. We have two other books already.

Okay. So, what have I covered so far? My wife. Her job. Me. And this journal. Maybe I'll think about the fact that there are no more wars. That global warming has been halted. And that cars are gone and everyone walks or uses electric trains. Then again maybe I won't. Everybody knows all that stuff.

I'd love to dole out some gossip, but everyone knows all of that, too. Hey, have you heard that the dairymen in ParisProvence are still refusing to pasteurize their milk? You have. Whoa, what about the news vids that dealers in Talibanistan are cutting their export heroin with dust? Every high school kid knows that. What about the suspicion that Mormons in UtIdaho are stockpiling antique guns? Already have that suspicion, though you—along with everybody else—can't picture how a five-inch guy with a beard can point—let alone shoot—one of those huge old weapons.

STEPHEN HOUSER

After Gen's call I yank off my Thinking Cap, shower away the dairy smells as well as my own manly man fumes, and get the hell to Washington before my window slams shut. I make it in time to enjoy an arousing adventure up the presidential creek with *my* paddle. An outing that I am especially fond of. It's probably the pope part of me. Looking for love in all the wrong places.

CHAPTER 2

I am snuggling Geness. Spooning her on one of the Oval Office sofas while she enjoys post-coital dreams. I'm looking around her famous workplace. This isn't the Original Oval Office, of course. It's a miniature replica that was made to suit the first Final-size president. He was elected some two hundred years ago and memorialized here by the bullet holes left in the walls after a failed assassination attempt. When I say Final—as in Original, Intermediate, and Final—I am using the official designations for the three sizes of humans that evolved during the Downsizing.

Nowadays, a lot of people just say Large, Medium, and Small, and though I find that a little too casual for my taste, it doesn't make me nearly as uncomfortable as the latest jargon, Venti, Grande, and Tall. This current fad even refers to the global Downsizing conflicts as the Starbucks Wars. Seems a little flippant to me. Given that some ten million soldiers died and more than twenty million robots were destroyed.

I search the walls until I find the bullet holes. A cluster of holes framed by dark-stained mahogany slats. Except for the military no one is supposed to own guns any more. Uh-huh. Actually, America *is* pretty clean. But people in places like DarkestAfrica routinely settle disputes by shooting each other to pieces. The United Nations rarely acknowledges such incidents, but the amateur vids that stream out of DA tell it all.

Gen turns her body and puts her arms around me. She smiles sleepily and puts her lips to my ear.

"Say something romantic," she whispers.

"Push your cooch against my dick," I whisper back.

Geness nips my nose with her teeth.

"How about another try?" she suggests.

"Did they save the Original Oval Office someplace?" I ask.

Gen takes her hand, grabs my chin, and turns my face toward hers.

"For a guy being offered seconds that fell a little short," she says exasperated. "And yes, they did. It's at the Smithsonian."

"Have you seen it?"

"I went there once after I was elected."

I begin to kiss Geness's neck while she speaks. If it affects Madam President she doesn't show it. Narced or not.

"It has real oil paintings on the walls," she says, "and built-in mahogany bookcases with antique volumes and historic sculptures. And get this," Gen says and her eyes go wide. "It has a wood-burning fireplace."

"What's so great about that?" I ask. "Everybody has a fireplace."

"Because we *heat* with wood. Before the Downsizing, Americans heated with oil and gas. The fireplace in the Oval Office was purely for decorative use."

TALL WAR

"Well, that's pretty decadent," I say getting Gen's point. Talk about showing off. The presidents sitting atop the crumbling republic still burned protected wood in a banned fireplace even as the remaining reserves of oil and gas were tapped to heat the Oval Office.

"Not only that," Geness says, "those last wastrels probably had the furnace *and* the fireplace going at the same time."

Now that's hard to imagine. But then so are throw-away plastic bottles and single-use metal cans. Yet we have some ten trillion cubic yards of landfill to remind us how real those were. Our American ancestors were unbridled consumers (*their* word) who fell just short of turning the whole planet into trash. Food for thought. Later. Right now, I am kissing my wife's neck like a fool who will not be denied.

"See that door to the left of my desk?" Geness asks.

"Yes," I lie. I don't even look.

"It's false. But the one in the first Oval Office was real and opened into a hidden room. Only the president could access it."

"Full of top-secret stuff?"

"Ha!" Geness laughs in a high, delighted chirp. "One of the presidents went there to pray. Another one snuck in his mistress for a blow job. One guy even kept his dead enemy's pistol in there to show to his buddies."

"Guess which guy I would have voted for?"

"I don't have to guess, Pa," Gen tells me. "I know you're a praying kind of fella." She throws her head back and laughs. She knows I'd pick the guy with the gun in a heartbeat. Geness calls me Pa when she thinks my conservative positions are just plain stupid. I'd like to call her Ma back, but it would fall flat. She's liberal, and she's smooth and glib.

I laugh, too, and pull Gen closer.

"How long does your pill work, snookums?" I ask, nibbling on her ear.

"It's not a pill. It's a suppository. And it's almost worn off. I can feel my anus starting to tighten up."

Christ almighty. Tighten up? That sends a testosterone-fueled message to my brain
in a desperate bid for the right romantic words to say.

"Geness, my love," I tell her. "Why don't you put your silky skin next to mine?"

I kiss her neck again and work my way up toward her lips. Geness turns and puts her ass against my cock.

"You are mine, darling," I whisper and slip into her. The next thing I know the president is panting out the national anthem.

I love politics.

CHAPTER 3

Afternoon delight with my sweet Geness came to a pleasant end and I caught an ElecT back to Falls Church, Virginia, the stop closest to my farm. ElecT, by the way, is the uber clever House of Representatives' name for the network of electric trains that connect all the parts of the US. Dumb name or not, it's a pretty handy way to go here and there in speed and comfort.

I walked home from the train station on an old dirt path that runs along a colonial-era canal. Hundreds of years ago it was filled with trash in a suburb surrounded by other suburbs. Now its waters run free through beautiful woods filled with wild game. And farmhouses and barns. And cows.

When I left Geness, she rushed off to shower and dress for a dinner with some congressmen. Actually, with *all* of the congressmen. Four representatives and eight senators. It's a small group and it's manageable. Something that could not be said of the old United States Senate and House of Representatives.

Back in the day, that Congress was filled with hundreds of battling, foul-mouthed partisans whipped into a perpetual frenzy by throngs of conniving lobbyists. Helps explain why what's-his-president prayed in his secret room and another one needed a blow job just to keep from going crazy. The fella with the dead guy's gun was already crazy, as far as I can figure.

Back at the farm I headed straight for the barn where the cows were waiting to be milked. I cleaned up when I finished and fixed some dinner for my son Lodge. He's a handsome, brown-haired, brown-eyed little guy of two years who devotes himself to computer screens of every size and eats in between vids. He's taken to running all over the farmhouse, but no one's heard him say any words yet. Haven't heard him say *Daddy* at any rate. He might have said *TV*.

Geness's mom, Corkabee, watched him today and told me all about it. In turn, I told her that Gen was working hard, but walking funny. Actually, I left the walking funny part out. Corky loves Gen fiercely, but even after seven years of marriage to her daughter there's something about me that makes her worry. She's the one who hooked me up with the perv suit, you'll recall. Geness has a healthy sex drive, but I'm thinking that maybe her mom doesn't. And that makes her suspicious of what Gen and I do when we're alone.

I wonder if Corkabee ever gets any from Wilson, her husband. Corky's a busty strawberry-blonde, and Wilson's a tall, bald-by-design, good-looking guy. She's forty-four or forty-five. Wilson is somewhere near fifty. Prime of life kind of people, yet neither one of them seems particularly vital. They look a bit diminished. Deflated. As though some of their hormones have leaked out. My bet is that it's been a coon's age since they did it.

Good God, people. There are drugs for that. In fact, there are drugs for everything. There's no excuse to be edgy, or horny, or worried about someone else's love life, even if that someone is your daughter.

When I was on the train coming home, I thought back on Gen's first days in office. I asked her then whether she got to see any secret government stuff that us ordinary nobodies didn't even know about.

"Oh, my, yes," she answered, putting down her coffee cup and eating her last bit of toasted bagel. "And I can't tell you anything."

"Did I ask you to?" I said offended.

"You were going to," she said looking at me. "I know you."

"Maybe," I admitted, picking up my own coffee cup and stewing about Gen's refusal.

"Like what?" she asked after a moment, bless her.

"Is it true that some Originals wanted to stop the Downsizing after its first couple of decades? Some TV programs claim that it was the spark that ignited the First Downsizing War."

"Sadly, that's true," Geness answered. "The Originals designed and implemented the Downsizing Program and the vast majority of them stuck with it. The last three generations of full-sized humans lived and died without having any children." Gen's face went sad. "Can you imagine that, Ben? A world without any children? How brave those people must have been."

Tears glistened in the corners of Gen's eyes. She wiped them away with the back of her hand and went on.

"The Originals faithfully executed the Downsizing requirements and strictly enforced its schedule as laid out in hundreds of thousands of ePages, and implemented it precisely over the twenty-generation transition period from Originals to Intermediates to Finals.

"There were problems, the most significant being the two terrible wars that delayed the end results of the Downsizing process by ten generations. The first conflict started twenty years after the Downsizing began. The ten most populous Asian countries formed a coalition with a block of twelve Arab nations.

"They built armies and constructed armaments for the express purpose of destroying the United Nations and preventing the planned extinction of full-size humans. The initial surprise attacks by the so-called League of Originals did huge damage to the United Nations' armed forces, but its remaining forces retaliated ferociously, and the ensuing war consumed entire armies and killed countless civilians around the globe.

"The war continued for two decades. Its longevity resulted in the evolution of the war where the United Nations' senior soldiers faced young, fanatical males being produced by the rebel nations. The UN Originals were saved from annihilation by clone armies composed of Intermediate-sized soldiers. These troops—though less than half the size of Originals—were physically enhanced specimens turned out by millions of UN labs all over the world. In the long run, their massive numbers defeated the armies of the League of Originals.

"After that coalition fell, the UN focused on a second Downsizing war, eliminating any remaining armed resistance. Drug cartels in Mexico. Unionized miners in South America. Mob families in Sicily. Generals in Myanmar. And the scores of mercenary brigades hired by wealthy families. Every last one of these rebel groups knew they would never be able to stop the Downsizing, but fought to the death anyway. Go figure."

TALL WAR

"They were all killed?"

"Totally wiped out. But at the cost of thousands of the Intermediate special army forces who tracked them down."

"Death squads?"

Gen frowned. Then nodded.

"The vids are gruesome."

"You've seen them?" I asked feeling jealous.

"Yes," Geness said, quietly. "While Intermediate humans were being bred to provide the next generation of soldiers replacing the Originals, the number of robots dedicated to maintaining the world's physical infrastructure was vastly increased in order to free up all medium-sized humans for war.

"Unfortunately, a clandestine group of American businessmen managed to bribe several key software design engineers to program backdoor access into the robotic software. Using that, countess robots were converted overnight into military bots and the third Downsizing War was launched. Millions of Intermediate soldiers died fighting outlaw bots, and countless UN robots were destroyed as well."

"But what about Asimov's Three Robotic Laws?" I asked. "You know, the ones about robots not harming a human or letting them come to harm?"

"That's science fiction stuff, Ben," Gen replied dismissively. "In the real world anything that can be programmed can be *reprogramed*. The rebel bots would have shot Isaac Asimov's ass off.

"At the end of the second Downsizing War there were fears that the Intermediates would refuse to stand down when it came time for them to be replaced with Final-size humans. But, in fact, they did their duty and phased themselves out of both their military roles and their governing positions at the UN, allowing the first generation of Finals to take over caring for and defending the Earth. The UN deactivated and dismantled all the remaining military Intermediate robots as well. And the Earth has not seen *any* fighting machines since that time."

My wife paused and looked at me.

"There's one more detail that I know about. We have saved the technology that was developed to create military robots. It is archived in a hidden location in Washington, DC."

"Who in their right minds would save *that*?" was all I could think to ask. My tiny little country was hiding tinder and powder that could blow up our entire new world. And if Gen knew about it—*and* the person who told her knew about it—how many others knew about this doomsday weapon?

"The world has been at peace for two hundred years," I whispered, dazed at Gen's revelation. "Why preserve something so terrible?"

My wife's face softened as she looked at me, and then it became truly anxious. "Because things change, Ben," she said, simply. "Things change."

CHAPTER 4

Geness called me last night when I was sound asleep. Didn't even have to open my eyes to see her face staring at me on my netacts lenses.

"Benedict, wake up!" she said sharply.

"What?" I asked, sitting up. I looked at the alarm clock. Two forty a.m. Piss and shit. Three hours before I had to get up to milk the cows. Geness was sitting at her desk in the Oval Office wearing a white terrycloth robe with a presidential seal. Her face was deadly serious.

"I need you to come to Washington *right now*, Ben," she said.

"Are you okay?"

"I'm fine, but I need you *here*."

"Lodge, too?" I asked, thinking I'd have to bring the baby along as well.

"No. I already called Mom and she's on the way over to the house."

"You called *her* before you called me?"

"Shut up, Ben, and get dressed." Gen's eyes narrowed and she clenched her jaws. "I need you here as soon as possible."

I'd never seen Gen like that before. Her intensity and her edginess had to indicate that something really big—and probably really bad—had happened. I shot out of bed and started pulling on my RediMedi suit.

"What's happening?" I asked, yanking up the zipper. Gen watched me dress, an expression of profound uncertainty on her face. I'd never seen that expression before. I wasn't sure if it was my wife who needed me, or the president of the United States.

"I can't tell you," Gen answered abruptly. "Just get here."

Ouch. If she was agitated now, she wasn't going to like what she was going to hear next.

"I have to milk the cows before I come."

"Oh, Christ," Gen swore. "I forgot about them." I stared at her face on my netacts. She wasn't agitated. She was panicked. "Something huge has happened, Ben. Please hurry. I wouldn't ask if it wasn't really, really important."

"Okay," I answered, trying to stay calm for Gen's sake. "I'll milk the cows early and catch the ElecT by 3:30."

"Thank you, love," Geness whispered. She sounded so appreciative I almost said to hell with the cows. But like kids, you don't just go off and leave them in need. "Call me when you're on the train," Gen said and hung up.

That was five minutes ago. When I walked out of the bedroom Corkabee was letting herself in the front door. She looked at me afraid and distressed. It was obvious that Geness had managed to get her riled up, too, without telling her what dire calamity had occurred. Gen had just hustled her out of bed and

TALL WAR

sent her over here. Corky's strawberry-blonde hair was uncombed and there were dark circles under her eyes.

"Thanks for coming," I tell her. "I'll make some coffee."

"I can do it," she says with the same edge some handicapped folks use when you offer to give them a hand. Okay then, Corky. Make the coffee.

I follow her into the kitchen. Corkabee gets the lights and grabs the coffee pot. Our farmhouse kitchen—which usually is a comfort to me—seems lonely. Everything reveals Gen's touch. But there's no Gen. In the center of the kitchen is a table with a butcher block top and four white, wooden chairs. Blue crinoline curtains with windmill appliques hang in front of the windows over the sink. Dutch wooden shoes lined up in pairs sit on the bottom shelf of a maple hutch in the corner, with blue Delft China sorted out on the middle and top shelves. I sit at the table and watch Cork.

She gets the coffee going and sets a coffee cup and saucer in front of me. She places another cup for herself across from me. I use a remote to flip on the 3D vid screen on the wall. The twenty-four-hour news stations are showing crop reports and livestock prices. Standard mid-summer television programming, yet it reassures me that whatever has gotten Gen all freaked out is not on the news yet.

"Geness told me she was fine," I say to Corky who is standing by the coffee maker watching the news. "Did she tell you that, too?"

"She did," Cork answers, keeping her eyes on the vid screen. "And she refused to answer any questions about what was going on. But obviously, there's a crisis." Corky frowns, then looks at me. Troubled that she doesn't know what emergency her daughter is facing. The coffee machine beeps and Corkabee picks up the glass pot and fills our cups.

My mother-in-law is plenty damn smart. And Carmel Wilson, her husband, is probably twice as smart as she is. Wilson works in the country's communications infrastructure, making the electronic skeletons dance as I like to tell him. Corky doesn't work. She mostly just takes care of her husband, which is good because Wilson doesn't really do anything *but* work. The man hasn't taken a day off in five years.

Corky sets the sugar bowl and a spoon in front of me and puts another spoon beside my cup. She sits down. I help myself to the sugar while she takes a sip of her black coffee.

"Can I get you some breakfast?" she asks and runs a hand through her hair. It doesn't make any noticeable difference that I can see.

"That would be nice," I tell her.

Corkabee looks at me for a long moment. Is she deciding whether she really wants to cook for me?

"What would you like?" she asks finally.

"Bacon and eggs would be great."

"Crisp and fried?" Corky asks.

"Perfect," I lie. I actually like light and scrambled, but I'm not going to jeopardize the longest stretch of niceness Corkabee has ever shown me.

Before Corky can move, she bursts into tears. She puts her face in her hands and lets it all out.

"Corky," I say softly. "Gen is okay, I'm sure she is. Everything is going to be fine." I know I should stand up and hold my mother-in-law, but she hasn't hugged me since I said *I do* to her daughter and Corky gave me a squeeze afterwards. Don't know why she keeps her distance from me. But I honor that, and I don't spend a lot of time worrying about it. Corkabee wipes her eyes with her napkin.

"I'm going to get the milking started," I tell her.

She nods and sniffs.

I get up and walk through the kitchen into the mud room. I pull on my boots, my beautiful black leather WyOkla cowboy boots. The toe box is covered with Nile croc. The vamp—as well as both front and back counters—are made from whole grain cowhide. There is foxing and decorative piping stitched all over the face of the boots.

When Geness and I first started dating she saw my yellow dairy boots made from some kind of fake rubber, riddled with holes where pieces had been torn out. She tossed them and ordered me my first pair of cowboy boots. I felt like a million bucks walking around in those. And three pairs later I still feel that same euphoria, wading through the daily toil of my job with my head held high.

I cross the backyard to the barn. It's an Original beauty, big and red. I have ten cows. All Holstein-Friesians. They are the black-and-white hybrids most people think of when I say I have dairy cows. Experience has taught me that if I call my girls by name and chat them up a bit, they will each produce an extra quart of milk every day. Go figure. It took me a while to get the right tone and the proper volume with each cow. I even had to work at how long I chat up each cow while I am milking her. Every cow has its particulars. Not so different from humans, eh?

I turn the lights on in the barn and give my beauties a few moments to get used to the fact that I'm early. Won't get as much milk at this hour, *and* I'll have to make sure I'm back again early tonight as they'll be carrying the extra milk I don't get this morning.

I wonder if I've put anything yet in my Thinking Cap about the fact that humans were the only species to be downsized? All the others were either weeded back, weeded out—I know that doesn't sound very nice, but it's the plain truth—or left on their own. Take dogs for example. They were all but eliminated except for some specialized herding and retrieval breeds. Cats, on the other hand, were left alone. They would be needed more than ever to hunt rats, mice, and other scavengers that fed on stored produce.

Most domesticated animals raised for US tables were assigned to specific North American nations for reproductive management, slaughter, and distribution. UtIdaho and WyOkla campaigned hard for a cattle concession, but they wound up with the two pork concessions and Montanada got the beef concession along with a wheat concession.

I am getting pretty far astray of what I want to say. Which is that my cows are Original size. That makes them as big as dinosaurs to me. Five feet tall at the shoulder and each one packing fifteen hundred pounds. They're my babies. All seven tons total.

I greet my girls and ask them how they're doing. Mostly grumpy this early it seems. But I'll dish out extra oats for breakfast as my way of saying thanks for humoring the old man. I climb the ladders in each pen, chit chat with the ladies, and then connect the needle-nose hoses to their udder splints that will suck out the milk and send it off to an assembly of Fullwood Packo machines where the milk is pasteurized, cooled instantly, and then sealed in sterilized 1/16th pint glass containers.

TALL WAR

Corkabee appears at the barn door. She's holding a plate of bacon, eggs, and toast for me. She looks a little calmer, but it's obvious that she's still upset.

"Wilson found out what's going on in Washington," she tells me, walking up and handing me the plate.

"And?"

"Don't piss yourself," she says not joking. "I almost did." Corky looks me straight in the eye, something she usually does not do unless I am under suspicion for a misdeed. I cower instinctively. "There's a spaceship in the Potomac."

I stare at my mother-in-law. I don't know what to think. I don't know what to say. So, I do what all young men do in similar circumstances. I repeat what she just said.

"A *spaceship* crashed in the Potomac?"

"It didn't crash," Corkabee corrects me. "Wilson says it was designed to land on water. To *splashdown*. It looks like it came in hard though and sustained some damage."

"On the Potomac?" I ask. My brain is not handling this news well.

"Yes. Near Mount Vernon." Cork stares at me as though pondering whether she should slap me one. Instead, she goes on. "Wilson thinks it's an American vessel. Like the ones used to colonize space. He found digitized vids of such ships from the twenty-third century."

Well, goddamn. My mental faculties finally kick in. I am amazed and frightened at the same time. A five-hundred-year-old American spaceship has landed on the Potomac River. Which by simple logic means that inside that ship are the first Originals to show up on Earth since the Downsizing.

With a little luck, they all died on impact.

CHAPTER 5

I get to Washington a little after four o'clock in the morning. I can smell the scent of the cherry blossoms. Most petals have fallen, but the rich Japanese perfume still lies heavy in the air. Summer is near with its heat and humidity. But for now, the final days of spring endure. Clean and scented with the sweet odor of cherry blossoms.

I walk around the Tidal Basin as the dawn becomes purple and orange in the eastern sky. I cross over to the National Mall noting the seam in the Washington Monument that marks the height of the obelisk when work stopped for twenty-five years. I turn and walk toward the back lawn of the White House. It is more of a park really, with trees and flowers everywhere.

In fact, Washington has been redesigned as a nature preserve. Only the White House and the Capitol Building have been maintained for government use. And the only private building remaining is the Original's first Smithsonian headquarters. Everything else is gone. Buildings. Plazas. Monuments.

TALL WAR

Everything has fallen away or been taken away in the last half millennium so that today, all one encounters is a pristine natural expanse filled with Virginia oaks, Maryland pine, and petunias, tulips, and roses. The Washington, DC, national park.

I let myself in the back entrance of the White House and walk to the Oval Office. The halls are mighty quiet. Filled with 3D vids of forgotten POTUS and FLOTUS types. Well, not completely forgotten. I recognize some early Originals like George Washington and Andrew Jackson. But most of the faces are a blur. Representing the days before Americans became as patriotic about their planet as they were about their guns.

The door to the receptionist's area situated in front of the Oval Office is open. I can hear several intense voices coming from the president's famous workplace. I walk in. Geness is standing behind her desk, dressed formally in a black suit and cream blouse. She looks calm, but everyone surrounding her—which appears to be most of Congress—is talking all at once about the spaceship that has helped itself to a slip on the Potomac. Gen is somehow managing to look like she is listening to everybody at the same time.

"Gentlemen," she says finally. "Will you be seated? My assistant will bring coffee for everyone. Please tell her how you prefer it."

The men begin to sit down and Wahina o 'Ava, a large Polynesian woman with a wonderfully pleasant smile, makes the rounds asking the president's guests what they would like. For all of their loud babbling just moments before, these same men ask politely if they might have a muffin, or a bagel, or even a cookie with their coffee.

I recognize Senator Bail Ren from Baltimore, Maryland. Ren is barely five inches tall with a perpetual squeak for a voice.

And there is Senator Todderick Blainer from Bristol, Virginia. He always reminds me of Dickens' Fezziwig with his cloud of white hair and amused expression. I spot Congressman Carroll Harry Lee of Richmond, Virginia. He is the famously tall and distinguished descendent of the American Revolutionary hero, Lighthorse Harry Lee. Old Lighthorse was famous for his bravery and equally so for his stupidity. In Carroll, Harry Lee's genes have stayed the course.

Rigging Nash is seated in a chair right next to Gen's desk. Not good. Has the UN ambassador forced himself into the government's discussion about the newly landed spacecraft? Or has he been invited at Gen's initiative? Even at this hour he is perfectly groomed. His thick salt-and-pepper hair is combed and hair sprayed and he is wearing a black RediMedi. He sits rigidly upright, communicating to someone outside the Oval Office on his netacts.

Nash sees me standing in the doorway. He scowls. I scowl back. He is always full of himself. Devoid of any concerns for others. I find him an unpleasant man under any circumstances. He glares at me as though I have toilet paper stuck to my boot. His stare is so intimidating that I quickly glance at both of my heels. Innocent. Maybe it's just *me* that he finds objectionable.

"Madam President," Nash snaps at Gen. "What is your spouse doing here?" He tips his head toward where I am standing. Not one of his hairs moves out of place. Don't often get to see someone whose hair is as stiff as their manners. Geness, however, isn't flustered by his deliberate rudeness.

"Gentlemen," she says, "I believe that you all know my husband, Benedict Katz. Ben has graciously volunteered to serve in Congress for the duration of our crisis." Much to my relief there are a few hear-hears uttered after Gen's announcement, and there are welcoming smiles on most of the congressmen's faces. Gen waves me in.

I walk over to her desk, a gleaming cube of seamless aluminum with a glass top. It was fashioned from the much-honored Apollo 11 command module that took the first American Originals to the Moon in 1969 almost a thousand years ago. It was given as a gift to the first Final-size US president by the Chinese who bought up all the scrap when the museums on the Mall were shut down and emptied out hundreds of years ago.

Geness gives me a peck on the cheek. "Coffee, dear?" she asks. What a pro. Smooth as silk. Who'd ever guess the other kinds of sounds I've heard come out of her mouth? I give her a little lewd wink. One corner of her mouth lifts the tiniest bit. I grin. Like I said, the woman's a pro. And how about her spontaneous introduction? Congressional volunteer.

I grin again and look at Nash. He ignores me, already onto another call on his netacts. His lips aren't moving. He's got the ultra-deluxe set of netacts lenses. Those that hook right into the optical nerve and access the brain for thought communications. I'd buy one—or get Gen to buy me one—but I heard that there's an autocorrect feature that deletes idioms, off-color adverbs, and offensive adjectives. Can't have that. I'm not Gen. I don't have to endear myself to anyone except her. Well, maybe my cows, too. So far though, they haven't yet started wearing netacts.

"Thank you for coming, love," Gen whispers. "Have a seat anywhere."

Wahina catches me as I walk by. "Nice to see you again, Mr. Katz," she says and smiles. "Black coffee with a scoop of sugar, right?"

"How big is the scoop?" I ask.

She cups her palms together. "This big," she shows me.

"Better make it two," I say. She cracks up.

I head for a vacant chair in the back of the room, nodding at congressmen as I pass. Except for Gen, there aren't any women in leadership roles. Though there is defacto gender equality throughout our world, there are still male attitudes held over from the old days. One is a mistrust of women in power. Even modern Finals with their emotions tweaked by DNA adjustments can still begrudge commercial and political clout for women. Very few women hold political office in America.

Gen's base of support rests on her popular political web log and the resulting network of contacts she has nurtured nationwide. Every American seems to know Geness, and most seem to admire her. Women *and* men. When she decided to run for president, she was opposed by an isolationist curmudgeon. She beat him handily. And the men here—who have volunteered for Congress—don't seem to mind having a nice-looking gal at the top. Especially one who makes sure that coffee and treats are served.

Rigging Nash looks up and addresses Geness again.

"So, Gen," he asks, an undisguised challenge in his voice. "What is your plan?"

Everyone stares at the UN delegate, dismayed at his deliberate disrespect. Nash does it, of course, to flaunt his diminutive view of both Gen and America's role in the world at large. He is a true UNer. He puts the world body first. America and every other sovereign nation second. That's one of the reasons the Security Council appointed him the United States ambassador to the United Nations.

TALL WAR

"Mr. Nash," Geness responds unruffled by his rudeness. "The space vehicle has been secured to the Virginia riverbank of the Potomac. Sovereign US soil the last time I checked." Gen pauses and locks eyes with Rigging. "The craft is being observed by local justices of the peace. I propose that we join them and witness the moment when the spaceship's occupants emerge."

Nash cannot believe what he's just heard. His face is suddenly as bright red as if Geness had slapped him. "I counter-propose," he shoots back in a self-righteous tone, "that you immediately transfer all responsibility for dealing with the unidentified flying object to the United Nations."

"For the record, Mr. Nash," Gen tells him, her voice firm and confident, "you can propose or counter-propose all you want. The fact is the spaceship has set down in *America*. If the crew was at all interested in the United Nations it should have landed on the East River, not the Potomac." Everyone in the room applauds loudly.

Nash jumps to his feet furious. "Then I will inform the president of the Security Council on my own authority," he declares in a huff.

"Do so, by all means, Mr. Nash," Gen responds. "You are only here as my guest. Effective immediately that status is revoked." Geness stands and faces the angry UN delegate. "You may leave."

Rigging stands rigid, declining to respond. He bites his lip and thinks about what to do. Geness has read him like a Kindle. She knows that the bastard wants to see for himself what's in the spacecraft on the river and she has played her hand well.

"If, however," Gen goes on, speaking in a clearly conciliatory tone, "you choose to contact the United Nations at a time on which we both agree, you may accompany us to the space vehicle's landing site."

"You are actually going to go there on your own authority?" Nash asks, still clearly amazed at her intention to do so.

"I've said that twice in the last few minutes, Rigging," Gen answers him with only the slightest edge to her response.

Nash remains quiet for the moment. Maybe he's afraid to go along. Maybe I am too. What if the spacemen come out with their guns blazing? Wilson told Corkabee that the vessel floating on the river is large enough to hold three full-size Originals. That's mindboggling enough without adding weapons and attitude.

Rigging finally speaks.

"I wish to be included," he says, "Madam President."

Gen nods. Nash sits. Coffee's served.

CHAPTER 6

I am in the president's compartment on a private government ElecT train heading along the Potomac River to Mount Vernon. There's an armada of fishing boats on the river. I hold Gen's hand and watch them out the windows. Most are commercial dories. But there are also dinghies here and there, with adventurous boys holding poles over the sides of their boat.

I had no idea so many people wanted to eat fish. This time of year, they're after the sockeye salmon grinding up the river to spawn at the headwaters of the Potomac. I can appreciate that single-minded focus to get home. Except for the dying part after you're done.

If perchance one of the salmon takes a lure, there are entrepreneurs standing on the banks of the river with horses and wagons who will—for a fee—drag the fish out of the river, butcher it, and cart the pieces wherever you want. It's lots of work, but there's no way around it. These fish are as large in our world as leviathans that swallowed sailors in the last.

I heard somewhere that back in the twentieth or twenty-first century fish farms replaced wild catch with domesticated fillets. A lot of farm ponds still produce fish yet today, even though the world's lakes and oceans have rebounded. UtIdaho has serious acreage devoted to farm salmon which, as you can imagine, are a hell of a lot easier to harvest than pulling a twenty- or thirty-pound wild sockeye out of the Potomac.

We leave the fishermen behind after a while and then I see the spaceship. Its size is staggering. I gawk like a moron while everyone floods over to my side of the car to look out the windows for themselves. The spacecraft is shaped like the nipple on a baby bottle. It's floating on a curved bottom that is at least twenty feet in diameter with a height that is roughly double that. It's painted white with black on the bottom, and I can see burn marks from its descent through the Earth's atmosphere. The ship is intact. And not only intact. The son of a bitch looks *new*.

We all stare at it, realizing that whoever wanted to use it to get here, got here, and now the capsule door could open at any moment allowing the Originals to climb out and blast away. Oh, God. I groan and Gen looks at me. I shake my head. I'm okay. Just wasting my last minutes of life dying the thousand deaths cowards like me experience.

Corky told me this morning that America's first space flights ended with water splashdowns just like this one. Capsules were launched on top of rockets full of fuel. Then the rocket was jettisoned. The spacecraft orbited the Earth, completed its mission, and returned, splashing down with its crew back on Earth.

Later US space vehicles continued to be blasted into space, but returned like airplanes, landing on big tarmac runways. Then the splashdown thing was brought back again when giant space vessels—having travelled through the solar system carrying detachable capsules—released them to return to Earth again. I stare at the huge space vehicle floating on the water. Where has it been? What have its occupants seen and done? And most important, what are they up to now?

Our group eventually musters the courage to leave the train and walk toward the spaceship. Gen holds my hand so tightly I have to flex my fingers to get her to ease up. I see that Rigging Nash is accompanied by his chief of staff, Adrian Modigliarty. He is a pale, dark-haired man whom I have always mistrusted.

Rumors of kickbacks, bribes, and laundered credits constantly surround Modigliarty, and you know the old saying, where there's smoke someone is burning evidence. There are, in fact, so many rumors about Nash's number two that any talk about him quickly moves from smoke to flames. Modigliarty notices me, then turns his attention to Geness. And why not? I don't have any power—except for the power of milking—and neither I, nor my cows, are of any interest to Nash's political doppelganger. Fine with me. Slimy prick probably doesn't even use cream in his coffee.

Rigging Nash also has two female bodyguards in his entourage. Both are skinny-as-a-rail ninja types. Nothing but bone, sinew, and muscle. They have shaved heads and are wearing squish suits, modified RediMedis that can instantly inject a body with massive amounts of narcotic uppers while simultaneously compressing muscle tissue to conjure up the fastest moving, hardest hitting security personnel on the planet.

What the hell is Nash doing with one, let alone two of those? He must have ordered them after he found out that he was heading out to see the UFO floating on the Potomac. I'd like to have heard that call. Get me two of your skinniest women, quick!

My father-in-law Carmel Wilson once told me that the old paper comic books published centuries ago featured female superheroes with spectacularly large breasts and hips. Well, I'm looking at real girl superheroes here and there's not so much as a curve showing or a nipple popping. On the other hand, that's not to say that the Original fems back in the day didn't have giant tits and come-fuck-me figures. How amazing would it be to see some of *those* ladies haul ass out of the capsule and go at it with Nash's bodyguards? Maybe there's a silver lining to all this, after all.

The unmistakable sound of helicopters breaks the silence. The horizon is swallowed by a sky full of military choppers with blue United Nations' flags painted on their noses.

"Rigging Nash!" Geness growls at him, losing control.

"I had no choice," he tells her, defiantly. Adrian Modigliarty instantly steps up next to Nash as if to intimidate Gen. Or to reinforce Nash in his role as spoiler. "This is bigger than your jurisdiction, Gen," Rigging goes on. "And you should have honored that."

Geness glares at Nash but controls her fury and doesn't reply. The truth has a way of being recognizable no matter who says it.

Some of the helicopters hover above the space capsule while the rest land in waves, putting down on both sides of the river. As jarring as the noise is, the occupants of the spaceship seem oblivious to it. At least no one throws open the hatch to see who's making all the racket.

Hundreds of United Nations' soldiers wearing silver, military-grade RediMedi suits and blue helmets with UN seals begin setting up a perimeter around the riverbank where the spacecraft is moored. It has been secured to land by industrial strength

TALL WAR

hawsers requisitioned from the fish mongers along the river. Still, it looks to me like one strong yank from the spaceship would dislodge them all. But who knows? The capsule floats on the Potomac, bobbing gently, millions of miles away from wherever it came.

A squad of soldiers approaches us, led by a tall, grisly-looking officer sporting a gray walrus moustache and two gold stars on his helmet under its UN symbol.

"I am General Weldon Wainwright," he says in a low growl of a voice. "United Nations Armed Forces." He pauses and drills us with an iron gaze. Is that supposed to impress us? I work with full-size cows. No six-inch general is going to intimidate me.

Wainwright looks at Geness.

"Are you President Jones?"

She nods.

"How long has the space vehicle been here, Madam President?" the general asks, sounding considerably more respectful than at first.

"A local justice of the peace observed it floating in the river sometime around midnight," Gen answers. "He called in other justices of the peace and they secured it where it is now."

General Wainwright nods.

"When did you arrive?"

"About a half an hour ago."

The general turns his gaze to the spaceship. I'm sure he is sending live vids through his netacts to UN headquarters in New York City.

"Madam President," Wainwright says, addressing Geness again. "Is there any intel on this vessel?"

Gen stares at the general, not really sure what he's asking.

"There is," I answer for her.

Wainwright looks at me, not with annoyance, but certainly with surprise that I answered his question, not the president.

"Who are you?" he asks, sounding a tad discourteous to my ear. "The press secretary?"

"No," I answer. "I am the husband. My name is Benedict Katz and President Jones is my wife."

Wainwright nods, then waits to hear what I have to say.

"Gen's father—" I stop and start over. "The president's father, Dr. Carmel Wilson, is an Information Services expert who supports our federal government's electronic infrastructure. He believes this ship matches descriptions of American space vessels that were used in the twenty-third century."

General Wainwright studies the ship intently.

"How did he get that information?" he asks.

"Wikipedia," I lie.

"The ship looks new," the general says in a tentative way.

"I agree," I say, as though my opinion matters. "But as the cliché goes, looks can be deceiving."

General Wainwright smiles. It's restrained, but it's still a smile. "Thank you, Mr. Katz. Are you part of Information Services, too?"

"No, sir," I respond. "Dairy services."

CHAPTER 7

The general grins and his eyes twinkle. He excuses himself and begins walking toward the Potomac to get a closer view of the spaceship. His soldiers deploy themselves in front of him filling up the green space between the general and the capsule. Most of them are carrying semi-automatic rifles. But some have oddly shaped weapons whose functions I can only guess. Laser guns? Communication disrupters?

Several helicopters hover in stationary positions over the spaceship, undoubtedly carrying firepower that a vessel designed for travel through space wouldn't be able to withstand for a microsecond down here on Earth.

The soldiers part for General Wainwright who walks to the riverbank. He studies the spacecraft. Talks to someone on his netacts. Then returns. He keeps a stiff military demeanor, but I can tell he is impressed. He's just viewed a forty-foot-tall ship that has crossed the universe to float on the Potomac. The general talks to Gen. I and the congressmen listen in.

"United Nations' intelligence confirms that this ship matches an American type of space vessel that was used during solar colonization efforts in the 2200s," he tells Geness. "Material analyses, however, reveal that the craft does not date from that era. It is a modern reproduction of what was originally designed to be a re-entry capsule. A module deployed from a larger ship to return spacemen to Earth.

"The UN does not possess a space vehicle tracking technology capable of penetrating the atmosphere. There is no way to confirm that there is a mother ship in orbit around Earth. But considering the limitations of the spacecraft that has landed here, experts believe that another ship—from which this capsule was launched—is very likely circling the planet."

A discernable shiver goes through the group of observers listening to General Wainwright. A ship large enough to deploy this module is orbiting our world. What? More importantly, what next? I ball my hands into fists to hide my own fear and stick them inside my pants pockets.

"Life scans of the capsule confirm that there are occupants inside," General Wainwright continues, tossing a bigger bomb into the middle of our group. "There are three Original-size travelers in the capsule and they're all—" The spaceship's door opens before Wainwright can finish. Geness grasps my arm and glues herself to me.

All of us back away from the spaceship shocked and alarmed, forgetting that we came here to witness this very moment. The vehicle door is pushed farther open. The black hole left in its place reveals nothing of what's inside the craft. Nor does anyone immediately reveal himself. General Wainwright lifts his hand and the soldiers raise their weapons. The helicopters above the spaceship pull into a battle formation, lining up their guns and rockets on the vessel.

A helmeted torso bigger than God emerges from the opening. Gen gasps. I gasp. It is an Original. The first that any of us has ever seen. A spaceman wearing a scarlet helmet with a dark visor and a spacesuit that matches the color of his helmet.

Everyone stares at the giant standing in the capsule doorway. It is mindboggling to see how tall humans used to be. How tall and how *big*. This spaceman must weigh as much as eighty or ninety Finals. If I weren't seeing him for myself, I wouldn't be able to imagine it.

General Wainwright starts talking with someone on his netacts. I'm sure he's sending vids to the United Nations Security Council. I wonder how many officials have just crapped themselves.

The spaceman appears to be studying the ropes tethered to his ship. Then he looks at where the hawsers are attached to the riverbank a few feet away. There's no way he can make it to shore without getting wet. He looks at the soldiers with their weapons trained on him. Then at the helicopters overhead. Finally, he just stands there, as though he's trying to figure out what to do.

He's wearing thick scarlet and black gloves that look like they're made of asbestos. And he has a braided utility belt of the same material with various holsters hanging from it. Tools? Gauges? Guns? Two black hoses connect his helmet to a black pack on his back, which I figure must be some kind of intake/outtake system supplying the kind of air he needs to breathe.

"If he's human," Gen says, asking the question that *just* popped into my head, "why is he still wearing his helmet?"

"I don't know," I tell her. "The general told us that the spacemen were the same size as Originals, but that doesn't mean they're human."

"Oh, God," Gen whispers.

"Well, let's find out," General Wainwright says, having heard our conversation. He orders one of his aides to approach the capsule armed with flame guns. In moments, a half-dozen men assemble, each one holding what look like six-foot-long metal pipes. Wainwright speaks to them in a low voice. They spread out before the capsule and light up their flame throwers.

Small yellow flames spit out of the barrels, then are honed by the soldiers to sharp orange and blue darts. The soldiers spread out and each one aims his weapon at the patch of grass in front of him. I can't tell what they're doing, but they work fast, and then step back in unison from the burn areas they've created.

I take Gen's hand and walk closer. No one stops us. The troops have singed letters into the sod facing the spacecraft. I can read them, even upside down.

ATMOSPHERE

21% Oxygen

78% Nitrogen

1% Argon/Helium/Carbon Dioxide

The spaceman stares at the words for a few moments. Then he slowly pulls the glove off his left hand. It looks reassuringly human though each finger looks almost as big as a Final's torso. He reaches his bare hand toward the sun. Does he feel its heat? He pulls off the other glove. Then he raises both hands, grips his helmet, and rotates it inside a metal ring built into the neck of his suit.

He slowly lifts the helmet over his head. He's human all right. Except he's a she. Blue eyes. Platinum blonde hair cut pageboy short. High cheekbones. And a beautiful nose. She looks at the foot soldiers, the whirling helicopters, the sun high in the sky. Her lips move and she addresses us in a pleasant female voice. Not too loud. Not too soft. Just right.

"Thank you for describing the gases in your atmosphere," she says. "Not only is your air breathable, but it is sweet and clean."

Her accent is different than ours, harder sounding and containing Semitic-like gutturals. Her tone is nasal and her cadence flat. But she's speaking English. And American English at that.

General Wainwright holds some kind of device up to his throat and speaks.

"Greetings, space voyager," he says, his voice amplified. "I am General Weldon Wainwright representing the United Nations of Earth." The giant space fem nods and waits for him to go on. "Please identify yourself and your port of origin," he says.

"I am Lieutenant Commander Susan Talbot," she responds. "Of the MSS John F. Kennedy.

NASAM spacecraft identification 101149. It is a space exploration vehicle equipped with this return craft, *Jon Jon*. Home port, Lewis and Clark Colony, Planet Mars."

Planet Mars? *Jesus!* Mars?

"Why have you come here?" General Wainwright asks straight to the point.

The lieutenant commander doesn't seem offended.

"Commerce between Mars and Earth was halted in 2215 followed by a communications blackout imposed by Earth's government. While it was not a priority initially, Mars' scientists eventually developed alternative vehicle propellants to replace Earth-origin fossil fuels. This breakthrough eventually led to the production of a space vessel capable of returning to Earth in hopes that the long, slow expiration of the world had somehow been halted and the planet saved. We manned a pioneer ship that was launched to find out. And we deployed its return capsule to land." The beautiful spaceman pauses and smiles. "And here we are."

Talbot stops speaking and carefully scans the array of humanity watching her.

"General Wainwright," she asks finally. "Where are all the big people?"

CHAPTER 8

Where are all the big people? Yes, the Original-size astronaut standing in the space capsule doorway really did just ask that. It's a fair question obviously. And for her maybe even a pressing one. On the other hand, I find it demeaning and insulting. Gen reads me instantly and whispers in my ear.

"Dad is sending me wikis on my netacts," she says. I frown. "I know you don't like Wikipedia with its publicly accessed info—"

"—with its *publicly messed up info*," I substitute.

"—but the entries Dad has forwarded all allude to the fact that the first spacemen selected for America's NASA programs were picked for their physical and technical abilities, *not* for protocol sophistication. Wilson thinks the same may be true for these Martian spacers."

"Ya figure?" I grimace. Where are all the *big* people? For Pete's sake. An astronaut from Mars who thinks like a grade schooler? What does that say about the other Martians still in the capsule? Probably not Ray Bradbury material.

Gen ignores me.

"Maybe you should tell her about our cows," I suggest. Gen looks at me, not happy. "You know," I go on, spreading my arms wide, "the big ones?" As much as I meant that to be a smart-ass comment, my cows will ironically wind up being the key to our future relationship with the giant girl standing in the spaceship doorway.

General Wainwright is speaking to someone on his netacts again. My guess is that he's asking how the heck he should answer Officer Talbot's question. Simply revealing that the world's human population has been permanently recreated as humans less than six inches tall might be tantamount to issuing an invitation to the Originals on Mars to move back here and kick our downsized butts.

No matter what options Wainwright's superiors are considering, the fact is they really have very few. Hopefully, opting to immediately blow up the Martian spaceship sitting here in the Potomac River isn't one of them. Wainwright's discussion ends and he answers Talbot's question the only way he can without giving away the planet. Namely, he asks a question of his own.

"Lt. Commander Talbot, are you the captain of your vessel?"

"No," she replies. "I am the communications and liaison officer."

What? A junior officer has been assigned to make first contact with the long-lost Earthlings? That blows my mind. Where in God's name is the ship's captain in this historic meeting between the inhabitants of two planets in our solar system?

Wainwright is scowling. He's got to be thinking that, too. Maybe in more crude terms. But he manages to respond in a restrained, diplomatic manner.

"You are charged with the dissemination of official information concerning your mission?" he asks.

"Yes," Talbot answers.

TALL WAR

"What is your purpose here?" Wainwright asks.

"I stated that already, General," Talbot replies a bit stiffly. "We have returned to the place of our origin, hoping that the Earth had not succumbed to the many environmental ailments that were actively destroying it when our ancestors left for Mars. I am so thankful that it has been saved."

"So then," Wainwright follows up immediately. "Having found the Earth salvaged—if you will—what are your directives?"

Now it's the space traveler's turn to ponder. Her fate and the fate of her fellow crew members might well rest on how *she* answers the general's question. The soldiers facing her are indeed diminutive, but there are a lot of them and they're ready to fire.

"Sir," Talbot answers. "I need to defer that question to my commanding officer. I am not trying to be evasive. I do not have permission to discuss mission objectives."

"I understand," Wainwright replies. "I request that you contact said officer now."

Talbot nods and disappears back into the space capsule, leaving the door open. It still looks like a black hole to me. Just because a good-looking blonde stepped out of it first doesn't mean that the spaceship isn't filled with men and guns that can do horrible things to us. Wainwright goes back to his online conversation with whoever is watching his netacts images and weighing what they're seeing. I turn to Geness.

"So, what do you think?" I ask, giving her hand a reassuring squeeze. It's not as good as a reassuring grope, but considering there's a crowd around us, it will have to do.

"She seems nice," Gen answers.

Having just witnessed the first exchange between Earth inhabitants and descendants of the space pioneers who colonized

Mars a half millennium ago, my wife says that she thinks their spokesperson seems nice. I suspect that in Gen's eventual Wikipedia autobio she will beef that up a little.

"And what did you think?" she asks me.

"I thought she was nice, too," I reply.

Lieutenant Commander Talbot reappears in the doorway of the capsule.

"General Wainwright," she says. "Allow me to introduce the captain of the MSS John F. Kennedy. Admiral Gary David Friedman."

Talbot steps back inside again and Friedman appears in the doorway. His helmet is off and like Talbot, he is dressed in a one-piece red spacesuit. He is a stunner. Hollywood handsome, he is leading man perfect with dark wavy hair, blue eyes, and a nose that Apollo would have traded his chariot to possess. Who selected this spaceman? The Mars Motion Picture Academy? Sheesh lareesh. The commander's hair is cropped close with a streak of white above his forehead. He has blazing eyes and a powerful presence.

"General Wainwright," the admiral speaks. He has a clear, tenor voice. "Greetings from the Lewis and Clark Colony on Mars. We have no plans, no objectives, and no weapons. Our only desire is to breathe the air and walk the soil of the planet of our origin. We have come in peace." He smiles kindly, then finishes. "General, I hereby request permission for me and my crew to come ashore."

"Permission granted," Wainwright answers formally and snaps off a crisp salute. Friedman stands rigid and returns the salute. "And Admiral," Wainwright adds, "welcome home."

***

TALL WAR

The general gives the order for the troops to stand down and calls in a request to the United Nations Corp of Army Engineers to construct a means of allowing the space travelers to exit onto dry land.

Welcome home, Wainwright had told Freidman. Wow. The power of that gets to me for a moment. Geness, too. She is sobbing, hugging me close. I can feel relief coursing through her body. So far, this potentially dangerous encounter between Finals and Originals has gone as happily as anyone could have hoped. I touch Gen's cheek. She turns her face to me. We share a kiss worth remembering when we are old.

Everyone around us is relieved. Even Rigging Nash has a smile on his face as he gazes at the spacecraft bobbing gently on the river. Standing at his side—where else?—is Adrian Modigliarty. But he's not smiling. Then I notice that both of Nash's feministas are gone and that he and Modigliarty are actually staring at the capsule as though they are looking for something. Or someone. Or them.

Oh, no. No, no, no.

CHAPTER 9

Nash's two security agents have disappeared and I'm positive that he is somehow trying to sneak them onto the spaceship. He and his Rasputin—Adrian Modigliarty—stand watching the floating spacecraft. What does Nash think he's doing? And who the hell authorized it? Am I hysterical? Not quite. I'm saving that for the moment the astronauts find out there's a pair of spies aboard the *Jon Jon*.

I tug at Gen's hand. She looks at me. I nod toward an empty spot a dozen feet away. As we walk there, I get a message on my netacts with my name at the top.

Katz, Benedict

Netacts User 15JUN613021NW95TH

SEAWAUSA15DEC75

UNITED NATIONS ADVISORY

TALL WAR

> Your netacts send and receive logs are being continuously monitored by authorized UN personnel. You may not under any circumstances discuss, describe, or detail in any manner or media format the events that you are witnessing today or may witness in the future on the Potomac River, bordering the grounds of former Fort Washington, Virginia, USA, until such time—if ever—you receive permission from the United Nations. Failure to comply with this prohibition will result in arrest and incarceration without the filing of formal charges for an indeterminate period. Current average term 10.6 years.

Well, crap. After I read the UN's warning on how-to-ruin-your-life-for-good—at least 10.6 years of it—I decide that I need to call my father-in-law Carmel Wilson.

"Gen," I say, whispering even though we've moved pretty far away from General Wainwright and his troops. "I am pretty sure that Rigging Nash dispatched his agents into the Mars capsule."

Geness stares at me, forehead wrinkled, eyes intense.

"They weren't bodyguards?"

"No. I think Nash specifically brought them to spy on the spacers."

"Oh, God," Gen moans. "You saw them go on board?"

"No," I admit. "But Nash and Modigliarty are both hanging around keeping an eye on the spacecraft, *and* neither one of his two muscle-ass ladies are anywhere to be seen."

Gen purses her lips and studies me carefully.

"So, you're guessing all this, right?" She looks at me like I didn't shower before asking for head.

"Geness, look at Rigging and Modigliarty." She does. "They're watching the capsule when no one else is. Not even General Wainwright."

Gen narrows her eyes and drills into mine.

"What *exactly* are you saying, Benedict?"

"I think you should tell General Wainwright about Nash's missing *bodyguards* and see what he wants to do."

Gen shakes her head.

"We can't do that. What if Rigging has orders from the Security Council?"

"Orders?" I spit out abashed. "Of course, he has orders! The next thing you'll be telling me is that he's actually a good guy."

"I'm not so sure he isn't," Gen says ignoring my histrionics. "I mean, what do any of us really know about these Originals? No one saw their capsule land. It just all of a sudden *appeared*. Maybe the United Nations has authorized Nash to try and find out what's going on by sending spies into the capsule."

Well, Gen's logic is all well and nice, but *whoever* sent them, two hyped-up, flip-of-a-switch, violent agents have apparently snuck onto Admiral Friedman's ship. How is he going to handle that if—no—*when* he finds out? Something tells me he won't be as understanding as my wife is.

"Gen, we need to call Wilson."

Gen looks puzzled.

"*My* Wilson?"

"Yes," I tell her. "Your dad. He was able to hack the transmission logs of the justice of the peace who found the spaceship—sophisticated multi-encrypted law enforcement communications—and he passed them directly to you. Maybe he can advise us *now*. I think you should brief him on what Rigging Nash is up to, and ask if any vids are being sent by the spies in the spacecraft."

"Is that even possible?" Gen asks. She looks numbed by what she is hearing. Yet another amazing software trick? Yes. You've been Googled again.

"Please call your dad and let's find out," I encourage her.

Geness blinks and brings her netacts online.

"I got a UN warning a few minutes ago that my netacts are being monitored," I tell her. "Did you get one, too?"

Gen waits, but nothing appears.

"No," she says.

Privilege of rank, I guess. Or the UN is *secretly* monitoring her communications.

Gen calls Wilson.

"Hello, Dad," she says when he answers. "I need you to use an ultra-secure line. This one is? Okay, good. Have you been monitoring the transmissions in the military zone around the space capsule? Yes? I know those are probably huge numbers right now, but I need you to check them all. I believe that Rigging Nash has gotten two security specialists onto the Originals' space capsule without their knowledge. I want to know if and what they've transmitted."

"I'm on hold," Geness tells me. She looks confident again. Whatever Wilson told her has made her feel in control once more. "Dad says that the US tracks all communications from secured areas and he can check the logs. However, he says the spies will be using blocked IDs and encrypted language, so it will take him a few moments for his search application to identify them."

Gen goes back to her call.

"Okay. I'll wait to hear from you. I love you, Dad."

Gen ends the call.

"Wilson says that his application isolated some twenty possibilities, which he will un-encrypt. He also is going to check for transmissions on the emergency frequencies reserved for the United Nations Security Council. He wants to see if Nash's actions were authorized by the UN."

"Who's the council president now?" I ask. Funny how I can't ever remember something like that. Something *important* like that. Moments like these make me realize how sheltered I am in my little dairy world. May I never have to leave it again.

"The Security Council's presidency is a rotating position that changes every six months. It is an effort to keep its powers bipartisan," Gen replies. "The current president is Dung Tro from Beijing, China."

"Call Wilson back," I tell her. "Ask him if he can also filter out and read transmissions from this location to Tro, to any and all parties in Beijing, and to *anyone* on the Security Council."

Gen shudders at the implications of the last part of that request, but she calls Wilson back and asks for the extra information I solicited.

"He said he'll check," Gen tells me ending the call. "He also told me that he'd just picked up a low-grade microwave signal originating from this area. It had no discernable ID and was sent only once."

"Maybe some kind of single-shot transmission?" I guess. "A yes or a no to a waiting party?"

"Possibly," Gen responds. "But to whom?"

TALL WAR

"It has to be Nash. Or General Wainwright to my way of thinking," I answer. "But it could be anyone. An alert tuned to a single frequency and aimed at a dedicated receiver could originate from something as small as a nanochip in someone's earlobe. Press it and off pops the alarm. If it wasn't Rigging or the general it could be anybody."

Gen looks at me suspiciously.

"My God, Benedict. You know a lot about these things."

"Spy vids on TV," I tell her truthfully. "Doomsday served up in a thousand 3D episodes."

"You learned top-secret communication techniques by watching vids on TV?" Gen looks skeptical.

"What?" I ask. "You think I just sit around and watch porn all day?"

She keeps a poker face.

"Pul-lease, woman."

Gen gives me a smile and answers Wilson's call back. She listens intently. Then she ends the call without a word and stares at me.

"The signal was sent from right here alright," she confirms. "But it was sent by the space capsule. Dad thinks it might have been meant for the orbiting ship."

"What?" I ask, fighting down instant panic. "Is there somebody up there, too?"

"I don't know," Gen answers. "What I *do* know is that the ship down here is talking to the ship up there."

Admiral Friedman has apparently sent a communication to a Martian mother ship. And whether or not there are more astronauts on such a vessel, the signal from Friedman has certainly been forwarded by that ship's communications to the Mission

Control people back on Mars. All that from one microwave ping. Given how much it eventually stirred up everything, one ping was more than enough.

CHAPTER 10

Geness and I go home feeling helpless. Corkabee greets Gen with a sympathetic hug, and two-year-old Lodge runs up and kicks me a good one in the shin. He turns and runs like hell. I'm just lucky he doesn't have cowboy boots yet. I frown and look up at Corky. She lifts her hands as if to deny any responsibility for that little treat from my son.

"Sorry," she tells me. "He watched ninja vids all day," she adds. I nod as though that makes sense to me. Kick your dad. He's a threat. We all sit down at the kitchen table to kvetch and drink some coffee when Wilson calls again. He has unencrypted a transmission that had to have been sent by Rigging Nash's spies. Its recipient was a security firm in McLean, Virginia. Wilson forwards it to Gen. She reads it aloud.

> Three spacemen. Eating and sleeping facilities only. Onboard computer scanned.

STEPHEN HOUSER

Appears to lack apps for weapon deployment, re-launch, or auto-destruct. But such programs may be hidden or embedded in judas files.

Rigging Nash's agents are not only inside the capsule, but they've hacked into its computers. At least we know what they've learned so far. The spacecraft is a sitting duck. No guns. No rockets. No nothing. And it isn't going anywhere. Anyone who's seen the capsule already knew that. But the spy transmission confirms beyond any doubt that the Originals came here intending to stay. Period.

"What's a judas file?" I ask Gen.

"A deliberately misnamed file that holds a hidden application," she tells me.

"So, you think it's one thing, but it's actually something else?" I interpret.

"Exactly," Gen nods. "It's a betrayer."

Corkabee stays for dinner and she and Geness make us Southern fried chicken, black-eyed peas, grits, gravy, and biscuits. While they're cooking, I do my afternoon milking, and then run around the barnyard playing with Lodge. It's the same ninja game as before only with cow pies added. My son winds his way around them as I stand stationary waiting for him. Then he puts his head down and rushes me—cow pies be damned—aiming to deliver another shin kick like the one that nailed me in the house.

This time I am prepared and dodge his kick. He tries again and I make sure he misses. And so it goes until I see that he is getting discouraged. Then, like every good dad in the world, I let him connect with one of them. He lands his shoe just under my pants cuff and his baby shoe manages to scrape off all the skin on my leg for about three inches.

Game over. I bend down to look at my wound and Lodge delivers a penalty blow to my other shin. My jeans protect my leg this time, but I have to hold Lodge in a bear hug until he settles down, which he does shortly. Though that is not the same as Lodge understanding that taking down the Old Man is a game I would prefer that he didn't play again. Lodge gives me a kiss on the check and runs for the house. Probably to get a treat and very likely say his very first words, *Daddy's a wus.*

Dinner is filling, but we're all so tense it isn't the treat that Corky and Gen meant it to be.

I help clear the dishes from the table and manage to wiggle out of giving Lodge his nightly bath by claiming I can hardly walk. Corkabee chuckles. And yes, since you have to ask, it did sound like an *evil* chuckle. I hobble out to the barn to work on the odd jobs I save for the occasions when my mother-in-law visits. No one bothers me. And there are no more calls from Wilson. All apparently is quiet on the Potomac. I toy with the idea of Googling for information about the old United States space program, but that might keep me up late and make getting up to milk early tomorrow morning too much to face.

Turns out I can't sleep anyway. Gen somehow manages to, but I wrestle my pillow. I want to get on that capsule. Not just to find the spies. I want to see what's in there for myself. Finally, I get up and brew a pot of coffee. I make some toast and drink a couple of cups of coffee.

I wonder if the spacemen drink coffee. Nash's spies noted that the capsule had facilities for dining. Wonder what they ate on the trip from Mars? Powders and pastes? Hydrated or heated? Crap rations either way. Probably the real reason the Earth Originals abandoned space travel back when.

Then it occurs to me that the spacemen may have used up their provisions. They might not have any coffee, or toast, or anything. Would they ask for help if that was the case? I drink another cup of coffee and think about that.

Just before dawn I get dressed and head out to do the morning milking. Greeting my girls. Climbing up and down the ladders. Opening and closing the shunts. Ensuring that the milk is sucked into the tanks for heating and cooling. I sit in an old maple rocking chair, the varnish on the seat mostly gone, watching as dozens of cases are filled with brand-new bottles of milk, then stacked in the refrigeration unit by service bots. That's all they ever do. And that's only for a few minutes twice a day. Maybe I can program them to kick Lodge.

I walk back to the farmhouse and gobble down some more toast and finish off the pot of coffee. Then I go and wake Gen. She sits straight up in bed, startled. I sit down by her and take her hand.

"I've been thinking that maybe the Martian astronauts might need some food," I tell her.

Gen looks at me bleary-eyed. Maybe I should have waited until she had woken a bit more. I lay down on the bed next to her and put my arms around her. She snuggles close and shuts her eyes.

"I think we should take the spacers some milk and cheese," I go on. "And if you can help me get past General Wainwright, I think maybe I can get Admiral Friedman to invite me on board the capsule."

Gen opens her eyes again.

"What is this really about, Ben?" she demands. "Satisfying your curiosity?"

"That, *and* concern for Gary Friedman and his crew," I protest.

"The answer is no," Gen says, tone flat and final. "Rigging Nash's agents are inside the capsule somewhere, and despite things getting off to a friendly start with the spacemen, we don't really know anything about Friedman or his crew. On the other hand…" Gen stops talking and studies my face for a moment. "If you *were* able to get into the capsule, it would give us a chance to see inside the spacecraft and maybe even get some idea as to what our visitors are up to, be it legitimate or—"

"—Or a load of cow shit," I finish for her.

"On which subject I know you are an expert," Gen responds.

"So, I can go in?" I ask cheerfully.

"No."

"Why not?"

"Because I don't have any guarantee that you'll come back out," Gen answers bluntly.

I have to admit that I've been thinking about that, too. Even if I am welcomed on board by Admiral Friedman, who knows what could go wrong inside that huge spaceship? And that's *besides* the danger posed by Nash's pair of spies already inside. Something tells me they kick a lot harder than Lodge. Plus, they probably have some martial arts training as to where to aim those kicks as well. For now, I don't try to counter Gen's fear of something awful happening to me in the space capsule. Can't do that until I get past that worry myself.

Geness gets out of bed, pulls on a fuzzy pink robe, and heads to the bathroom. Frustrated, I go back to the kitchen and make another pot of coffee. It's ready when Gen walks in and sits down at the table. I fill up a mug for her. Whereas I take a lot of cream and sugar to cover the taste of coffee, Gen drinks hers black. Might be her only flaw.

"Okay," she says. "I think you and I should donate milk and cheese for the astronauts. And I will find people to donate fresh vegetables, fruit, and bread." Gen pauses to think for a moment. She props her chin on her left hand and slowly drums the table with the fingers on her right. "So, who's that going to be?" she murmurs to herself.

I fix her some toast and spread some apple butter on each slice. She likes it that way. Gen nibbles silently while she noodles on possible folks to help out with food for the space crew. From time to time, she scribbles some notes on a paper napkin, and after a while I refill her coffee.

"I'll approach Ees Barne about providing bread," she tells me at last. Ees is a senator from Harper's Ferry, West Virginia. Mild as snow, he has access to a grocery store chain on his wife's side. "And I'll talk to Cooley Firewall about vegetables and fruit." Cooley is also a senator, from Pike Creek, Delaware, and has ten thousand acres cultivating onions, cucumbers, squash, pumpkins, corn, green beans, and so forth. Plus, another five thousand acres of fruit orchards. Gen points at the apple butter on her toast. "That's from his farm."

I don't like apple butter. First, it's not real butter. And second, I *have* real butter. What person in their right mind would eat apple butter with tubs of sweet cream butter fresh from the dairy sitting in the cooler?

Gen goes on.

"After I get their commitments to help, I'll contact General Wainwright and tell him we're bringing food for the astronauts.

It will be a hell of a lot harder for him to tell me no if things are already rolling."

"Easier to ask forgiveness than permission," I agree. My father used to whisper that to me when we were sneaking cigarettes together behind the barn. On the one occasion when my mother sniffed out our criminal activity, my father was right. She did forgive us. She also took dessert off the dinner menu for a month. No smoke was worth that. To this day I know that if I wind up in front of a firing squad and am offered a last cigarette, I'll ask for a piece of pie instead.

"So, that's the plan," Gen says looking pleased with herself.

"Great! How about if I'm the one who tells Admiral Friedman about the food?"

"So you can finagle an invitation into the capsule?" Gen accuses. She shakes her head. "No."

"I think *yes* is a far better answer."

"But the answer is *no*."

"Five minutes ago in the bedroom you were willing to consider it," I whine.

"There are a lot of things considered in a dark bedroom that never see the light of day, Benedict." My wife, the psychologist. Or sexologist.

I frown.

"I'll ask you later," I say in a pouty voice. I finish my coffee and stand up.

"Not so fast," Gen tells me. "You woke me up pretty early. There's a price to pay for that, *hombre*." She reaches into her bathrobe pocket and takes out a pill. She tosses it in her mouth and swallows it with the last of her coffee. She stands and drops her robe to the floor. I look at her pink nipples and heavy breasts.

"I just took a PopPop," she says, a sultry tone to her voice. "Proof that *some* of the things considered in the bedroom *do* get acted on."

I stare at my wife in disbelief. A PopPop? That's a nerve enhancing drug tailored to stimulate female genitals to multiple orgasms.

"You took a PopPop?" I say not believing it. Unspoken, but implied by my offended tone are the words, *You want sex after giving me nonstop crap about getting into the capsule?*

Gen steps close and puts her arms around me. She licks her lips with her tongue. "Yes, I did. Right in front of you so you would see me do it. With a little co-operation from you, lover boy, maybe my *no, no* about entering the spacecraft will turn into a *yes, yes.*"

Gen licks her lips again.

"Kiss me," she says. She points at them. I kiss her. Then she points at one of her nipples. Ditto. She points at her naked pubic area. Over the next few minutes Gen moans out her homage to pharmaceutical technology with a whole series of pops. Reminds me of a string of firecrackers on the Fourth of July. God bless America. And God bless its president.

CHAPTER 11

*Making a list, checking it twice,
gonna find out who's naughty and nice.*

I thought that song was full of crap when I was a kid. Didn't believe in Jesus. Didn't believe in Buddha. Sure as hell didn't believe in Santa Claus. But I'm humming it like a whizbang now. Makes a difference when *you're* the one making the list.

64 1-ounce loaves of bread donated by Ees Barne. Nice
32 ounces of apple sauce donated by
Cooley Firewall. Nice.
32 ounces of cheddar cheese and 64 ounces
of fresh milk.
Donated by yours truly. Nice. Twice.

It all adds up to about forty pounds of food and that's not counting the vegetables Cooley has promised to bring later. Gen's off to the Oval Office working on getting the food picked up and delivered. She's trying to rope Senator Alasherm Lan from Sharpsburg, Maryland, into taking on that responsibility.

She called me earlier to tell me that General Wainwright had given permission to take the fresh food to Friedman and his crew. And she reminded me that he wouldn't have approved unless *he* had been given a thumbs up from the UN. That's good. It means that the initial reaction in New York is to hold out an olive branch to the folks from Mars.

Speaking of approval, I did get permission from Gen to try and talk my way into the space capsule. I pounced hard on the heels of her last pop. She sputtered out yes, but her eyes—even half-closed—were pissed. I don't feel guilty. The sex was her idea.

I catch the noon ElecT from Falls Church to DC and make a connection to Mount Vernon at the station where the old Lincoln Monument used to stand. It's hot out, but the sky is blue and the air is pure. Thanks to the Originals who made this happen, the whole planet can say the same. I am crossing my fingers that their newly arrived descendants will turn out to be as wise. It's too early to make a judgment. But it's not too early to be watching out for trouble. As the old saying goes, one bad udder can spoil the whole bucket.

Wilson called Gen again before she left home this morning. He'd been monitoring Security Council communications about the astronauts, but insisted on disguising what he'd learned because he wasn't sure how secure the White House phone lines were. He talked to Gen about the various ways an exterminator recommended dealing with the "rats" that had appeared in my barn. Gen understood. I understood. I have to say, though, that I was not too keen on anyone who might be listening in thinking that I had rats in my barn.

Anyway, Wilson told Geness that there had been a lot of discussion at the exterminator's headquarters. One expert favored quarantining the rats. Three others favored immediate elimination. The last member of the group thought that maybe the rats had a place on Earth, and that maybe we should just live and let live. Truth be told, as much as I like the sound of that last option, I can't figure out how we would ever make it work. Live with rats? Really big rats?

When I get off the train at Mount Vernon, I can see that the Potomac riverbank where the spaceship is tethered has been enclosed with barbed wire. The area beyond it is filled up with tents, soldiers, and equipment. A new road runs right up to the spaceship, and there is a steel platform under construction at the edge of the river with a catwalk that extends to the spaceship itself. Man, is there anything these guys can't do? Maybe I could get a few of them to stop by and fix the holes in my barn roof. Right. When dairymen fly.

A single metal gate in the barbwire fence opens into the enclosure. It is manned by two Marines. I walk up and they watch me approach. One of them with sergeant's stripes on his sleeves politely asks if he can help me. I tell him my name and ask to see General Wainwright. He asks to see my eDocuments. I bring up the ID file on my iAll and hand the device over.

United States law requires that any personal eInformation being inspected by American or UN authorities must be displayed on a monitor large enough for the citizen to observe what is being examined. The non-com complies with this law, wirelessly connecting my PDA to a larger screen on a work table set up inside the gate.

I watch the monitor as he flashes my life before my eyes. Birth certificate. Inoculation records. Occupation files. As well as tax records, health exams, medical consultations, psychiatric evaluations, and on and on. Only when he's finished with all of that does he look back up and ask *why* I want to see the general. I tell him that I have organized a food drive on behalf of the space crew that has been approved by both the United States government and the United Nations. At that the Marine puts in a call to General Wainwright.

He hangs up, motions me through the barricade, and escorts me to the general's tent. The flaps are open and I can see Weldon Wainwright working at a field desk surrounded by staff personnel. The general looks up and beckons to me. He stands and shakes my hand.

"Mr. Vice President," he says.

"General, I'm not—"

Wainwright puts up his hand to stop me. "Please. Allow me my little idiosyncrasies." He smiles pleasantly. "You *should* be the vice president, though," he adds.

I blush.

"Have a seat," he tells me. "Cup a' Joe?"

"Sir?"

"Coffee?"

"Please."

"Usual poisons?"

"Yes, thank you. Sugar." I hope that's what he was asking me.

Wainwright waves a young aide over. "Two coffees, son. One with cream and the other with sugar." The soldier salutes and leaves the tent. The general sits back down. "A cargo truck arrived here early this morning with the milk and cheese from your farm. Another truck just showed up with fresh bread. So, all we're waiting on are the fruits and vegetables." The general gives me a you'd-make-a-good-soldier kind of smile, respectful and pleased. He's not recruiting me, but he is definitely letting me know that I've passed some kind of muster in his book.

Our coffee arrives in big white ceramic mugs. Steaming hot and black enough to swallow a constellation. The general is served. Then me. The aide leaves a tray with a sugar bowl, a creamer, spoons, and napkins.

"Help yourself," the general tells me and nods at the tray. I reach over and spoon sugar into my coffee. "Mr. Katz. I have to tell you that your food collection project is a first-class idea. Really smart. Taking the initiative to step up and address our visitors' needs is a powerful way of saying 'We mean you no harm.'"

"Even if we do," I reply. General Wainwright arches an eyebrow. I'm not being a smart ass. I'm just poking to see if the general is bullshitting me or is actually in favor of giving a break to the three Martians bobbing in the space capsule. He refuses to take the bait. I change the subject.

"I noticed that your engineers have gone to town getting that landing thing, that, that big,

big—" I struggle trying to find the right word for the structure that is being erected next to the spaceship.

"Thingamajigger?" the general offers.

"Yeah, that. It's big."

"It is, isn't it? When it's finished, we'll palletize the foodstuffs and have them transported onto the—" General Wainwright pauses.

"Thingamajigger," I offer.

"Yes," Wainwright grins. "That."

I nod. Then I spring my request.

"General, I would like go aboard the capsule when the food is delivered."

Wainwright stares at me.

"Why?"

"I want to see what's inside."

The general stares at me some more. I can see that he is chewing on my request like a piece of gum. Working it to see if there is enough flavor to interest him.

"Do you know anything about electronics?" he asks. We look each other in the eyes for a long moment.

"Are you asking if I would be able to recognize any of the data systems inside the spaceship?" I want to know.

No use beating around the space capsule. Does he want me to spy on the spacemen's equipment? Not that I would be the first. But Gen won't let me talk about Nash's spies yet.

The general nods.

"Bingo," he says.

"It's old stuff, right?" I ask. "Probably not as complicated as my dairy equipment."

The general raises his eyebrows. Surprised at my somewhat flippant take on our visitors' space technology.

"Do you think you could get three of your cows to Mars?" he asks, poking me, but not unkindly.

"Well, no."

"Then let's respect what it took the folks on Mars to get these three space voyagers here," Wainwright says, sticking it to me without humiliating me. "These astronauts have been gone from their planet for nine months—maybe more—and the shortest distance they could have traveled to get here was some fifty million miles. I, for one, would like to know more about their landing module. And whether it is, in fact, exclusively a descent vehicle originating from a mother ship orbiting our planet." The general looks directly at me. "Do you think you could help me out with that?"

"Is that your way of asking me to transmit vids from inside the spaceship?" I ask, already willing to do so.

"It sure is," Wainwright confirms.

"That wouldn't be a problem for me."

Wainwright nods.

"And how would you feel about getting requests on your netacts asking you to focus your transmissions on a specific feature? Say a close-up view of an instrument panel?"

"I'd do what I could to meet that request."

Wainwright nods again. Then goes for the jackpot question.

"Is there anything that I or my staff might ask you to vid that you *wouldn't* do?"

I answer without hesitation, "Not a thing."

The general looks at me and smiles a thin smile.

"You're in."

CHAPTER 12

"Why don't you come, too?" I ask General Wainwright.

He shakes his head.

"I can't tell you how much I'd like that," he answers. "But I can't. If the visitors turn hostile for any reason, they'd have a top-ranking UN military officer on their vessel. I can't risk any exposure of my core memory."

"Understood," I say and nod. I'm safe because *my* core memory is mostly about cows.

"Are you ready to meet Admiral Friedman?" he asks.

"Yes, sir." I try not to sound anxious, which I suddenly am.

General Wainwright stands up. So do I, adrenaline leaking out of my ears. I'm surprised that my RediMedi hasn't already patched me with a dose of Valium. Then I remember that when the suit discerns a fight-or-flight reflex in its wearer, it delays dispensing anything until it's obvious which option has been chosen. Fact is, I'm nowhere near fight-or-flight. I'm still in the why-the-hell-did-I want-to-do-this mode.

Wainwright tells one of his aides to have a car brought around. Then he leads me out of the tent. A military vehicle arrives that looks like a camouflaged convertible. I'm sure we'll blend right in with that. The general gets in the front next to the driver. I hop in the back and off we go.

As we approach the spaceship, I can see that the catwalk reaches all the way from the new steel gantry to the capsule door. We get out of the car and climb a set of steps to the top. There's an adjacent set of stairs big enough for the astronauts. General Wainwright leads me to the catwalk. It is wide and suited to the Originals. The spaceship's hatch is open. A soldier hands both Wainwright and me voice amplification devices. Wainwright holds his up to his throat.

"Admiral Friedman?" he asks. The general's voice is amped up significantly, but it's
not unpleasantly loud. Will Friedman hear it? "Admiral, this is General Weldon Wainwright requesting a meeting." The general and I wait. We shift back and forth in our boots. Wainwright in his standard military leathers and me in my custom WyoCo&Nebraska croc-tipped cowboy boots. Squeak, squeak, squeak go my boots as I wait. I take comfort in that down-home sound.

Gary Friedman appears in the capsule doorway. He is bareheaded and wearing a comfortable-looking blue flight suit unzipped at the neck. He salutes. Wainwright responds in kind.

"Good morning, General," Friedman says cordially.

"Good morning to you, too, Admiral," Wainwright responds. "We've brought fresh provisions for you and your crew."

The admiral's face lights up.

"By God, that's great!" he exclaims.

The general nods at me.

"This is Benedict Katz, Admiral. He organized the effort."

I hold the voice amplifier to my throat and talk.

"Pleased to meet you, sir," I say. "There is milk in vacuum sealed bottles. Fresh bread. Cheese. And apples rendered into sauce and delivered in squeeze bottles."

A wistful expression crosses Friedman's face.

"Mr. Katz," he says, "I have to tell you that I am touched. On Mars we raise and consume just about every kind of fruit, vegetable, and grain that you could imagine. However, we've never had dairy. Just a whiff of real cheese would probably be enough to raise the dead on Mars and have them clamoring to board the next ship to Earth!"

The general smiles. But I can tell that Friedman's comment about more ships coming from Mars instantly set him on edge.

"With your permission, Admiral," Wainwright responds, hiding the wariness I saw, "I'll have the foodstuffs brought to your ship. I have been assured that the foods are free from blight or disease and have been irradiated to ensure that all the surfaces are sterile. However, we do not have data on what kinds of microbes or bacteria your bodies can tolerate. You'll have to trust your best judgment as to what you decide to consume."

"I appreciate your thoroughness," the spaceship skipper replies. I realize for the first time that Friedman is talking much more softly than he is probably used to so that his Original-size voice won't hurt our ears. His thoughtfulness doesn't hide the fact that he has a melodious and smooth tenor voice. It would have been called a radio voice according to the archived videos I've watched about the early decades of the twentieth century. The first radios were primitive, having the technology to broadcast sound, but nothing more.

"Our remaining provisions are limited and are dry or dehydrated," Friedman tells us. "Fresh foods will be a wonderful treat. As to what we'll consume, General, I suspect we'll eat everything and just see what happens." Friedman grins and so do I. Ben Katz's down-home translation of the admiral's plan: We'll try it all and see who gets the shits.

"When shall I have the food transported?" Wainwright says.

"Anytime," Friedman replies and smiles.

"Then let's do it," the general says.

Wainwright leads me back across the catwalk and down the platform steps. I'm feeling like I really scored with my food-for-the-space-guys idea. I can't wait to have Admiral Friedman try his first bite of cheese. I stop dead. Wainwright stops on the steps below and looks up at me.

"What if the spacemen are lactose intolerant?" I ask him.

The general nods.

"Good point. Let's get the food up here and use that caveat as the means to get you invited into the spaceship."

I nod back. Caveat? A vice president might know what that means, but I sure don't.

The food has been packed in ten large wooden crates, each a foot square, each weighing about four pounds. That's an enormous amount of food by Final standards. But it's probably just a good start for the three Originals. General Wainwright has his troops hoist the crates onto the top of the platform. Then they carry them across the catwalk right up to the capsule's open hatch. We follow the soldiers and wait outside the *Jon Jon's* door.

"Admiral Friedman?" Wainwright calls out holding the amplifier to his throat. The *Kennedy's* skipper appears in moments. He is obviously pleased to see the crates of food. General Wainwright takes that as his queue to make the pitch he tried out on me earlier. "Mr. Katz would like to discuss some possible digestive concerns with you and your crew, Admiral," he says sounding very matter-of-fact. "Would it be possible for him to come aboard while you examine the various foods?"

"Absolutely," Friedman responds. "It would be an honor to have Mr. Katz as our guest. If you'll allow me just a minute to take the food in, I'll be back."

The admiral reaches for the boxes and picks up several of them, impressing both Wainwright and me with just how big and strong he is. He takes them inside and returns. In three trips he has taken them all. When Friedman finishes, he looks at me.

"Would you like to come aboard now?" he asks.

I look at the general.

"Go for it," he says.

Friedman puts his palm down and without having to be told I climb on.

"Shit howdy," I blurt out as the admiral lifts me up.

General Wainwright waves.

"Shit howdy?" Friedman asks.

"Dairy jargon," I tell him, and wave back at the general.

CHAPTER 13

Admiral Friedman lifts his hand slowly. I hold on.

"Are you doing okay?" he asks.

I nod. Never been this high before without a cow titty in my face. I blink and bring my netacts online. I have preset the mode so that whatever I look at, General Wainwright will get a live feed of what I'm seeing. Friedman steps down a ladder attached to the interior wall of the space capsule.

It is much darker than I expected. The only natural light comes from a long, curving window above the ship's dashboard. That and what comes in the open hatch. Three large reclining seats face the dash, padded and molded to protect the astronauts during re-entry. Behind them, a work station is molded into the capsule wall with recessed computer screens and built-in padded stools. Above the monitors are three long, recessed cubbies accessed by a vertical set of steps set into the wall. Sleeping bunks?

The admiral notices me checking them out. "Officer Talbot has rack time," he says, nodding his head upwards. "And here," he says, tapping the workstation surface, "is where we eat and do just about everything else. Officer Malcolm Saint Jean is using the head over there." Freidman nods in the direction of a closed door on the right. "I'm going to set you down and find something for you to sit on."

I step down from Friedman's palm onto the workstation. I scan the interior of the capsule again, providing Wainwright with vids of what I see. I am also secretly searching for Rigging Nash's two spies. I'd like to believe that they vacated the spacecraft after hacking the onboard computers for information. But I can't be sure that was their only mission. If they are still aboard, they could be hiding anywhere in the capsule. It's a hell of a lot bigger than Jonah's whale, with lots of room for stowaways.

Friedman returns with a small, silver-colored, rectangular metal box. He sits on a stool and holds it out for me to see.

"It's called a Zippo," he says. He holds it upright and tips back a lid with his forefinger. Inside is a mechanism topped with a wheel and wick. The admiral spins the wheel with his thumb and sparks light the wick. Whoa. A nice-sized flame appears, apparently drawing fuel from inside the lighter. Friedman closes the lid and lays it flat on the table.

"Hot stuff," I comment and sit.

"People used these to light cigarettes."

I frown confused.

"Rolled-up paper tubes filled with tobacco. They breathed in the smoke," Friedman explains. "Apparently it was much more pleasurable than it sounds."

I just shake my head.

The admiral chuckles.

"So, Mr. Katz," he says, a twinkle in his eye. "Just how *official* is your visit?"

"I'm just a dairy farmer," I tell him. "I couldn't be official even if I tried."

Friedman smiles appreciatively.

"Is this your first time in a spaceship?"

"Yes, sir. We don't have spaceships."

"Well, that's kind of sad," Friedman says. "Don't you think?"

"I never thought about it really," I answer. "Guy my size sees the Earth as pretty big. I don't have much interest in thinking about the endless distances of outer space."

Friedman smiles again.

"I like you, Mr. Katz."

"You can call me Ben, if you want."

"Great. Thank you, Ben. I'd like it if you called me Gary." Friedman smiles and rocks back and forth on his stool for a moment. I don't know much about psychology, but I'd say the admiral's inner child just got happy.

"I asked to come on board," I tell him, "to warn you about a potential digestion issue concerning milk and cheese. Since you and your people have never eaten milk products, your systems may have difficulties digesting their enzymes. This is also a common problem on Earth, though everyone drinks milk and eats cheese from the time they were kids.

"If any of you have issues, you can expect stomach cramps, gas, and maybe diarrhea. You and your crew might want to try a few bites of cheese or drink some milk and see how you do. Or, I can get you some supplements that will prevent the negative effects of being lactose intolerant."

"That's mighty thoughtful," Gary says. "I think those pills might be just the thing. Do they have any side effects?"

"None that I know of. I'll ask General Wainwright to get what you and your crew will need."

"Thanks, Ben. And let me thank you again for rounding up the fresh groceries for us.

I imagine it was quite a bit of work to do to make it happen."

"People were happy to help out," I answer truthfully. "Everything is organic and whole, though the apples delivered today started out Original-size before they were mashed into sauce for easy transport."

Admiral Friedman stares at me for a moment.

"When you say *Original-size*, Ben, what exactly do you mean by that?"

Oh, man. Gary's question raises all kinds of issues I don't think I should talk about. Anxiety rockets through my brain like a lightning bolt. My RediMedi suit reacts and patches me with an instant dose of Valium. I feel a slight tingling on my neck under my suit collar. Oh. Yes. My calm is *really* calm.

"Apples are the same size today as when Original-size humans were still around," I answer Gary.

Oh, my God. I blabbed. Utter panic voids my Valium and I break into a sweat. I can see that Friedman finds my answer stunning. However, he also sees my obvious discomfort and cuts me some slack.

"How about that?" is all he says.

"We tried to bring enough food to last several days," I tell him, trying to calm myself down again. "And we can bring more. Maybe we'll even try to rustle you up a barbeque." Did I just say barbeque? Either my nervousness or my drug is short-circuiting my brain.

TALL WAR

The admiral studies me for a moment. "Barbeque," he repeats. "Are we talking beef steaks cooked on a grill and slathered with spicy sauce?"

I nod.

"You could do that?"

I nod.

"My," Admiral Friedman says clearly impressed. "Is there any way you could save the cowhide so I could have a pair of boots like yours?"

I stretch out my legs and click my heels together.

"Maybe so," I tell the admiral. "Maybe so."

Friedman claps his hands and laughs.

"Shit howdy!"

CHAPTER 14

"Would you like some tea?" Gary asks me. He smiles pleasantly, completely masking any curiosity he might have about what's happened here on Earth over the last five hundred years. If I were him, I would be *so* jonesing to find out why the hell the human race was miniatured after his ancestors left for Mars. But he's not pushy. Which I appreciate.

For the first time I wonder if the admiral's own jumpsuit is, in fact, an offworlder's version of a RediMedi. Ready to dose its wearer with everything from sedatives to uberstimulants. Oh, yeah. Plenty of sex meds, too, I'd guess, though why a person would ask for those with their suit still *on* is beyond me.

On the other hand, maybe Friedman is the consummate military professional. Stay calm and carry on as the now Brits used to say. Professional or not, Wainwright—who has been watching my live vids—senses Friedman's curiosity, and opens a new screen on my netacts lenses and authorizes me to give the admiral a layman's spin on what happened with

TALL WAR

Downsizing and all. I assume by layman he means dairyman, so I go ahead.

"I *would* like some tea," I answer. "Thank you."

"How do you take it?" Gary asks.

"With sugar?" I ask, tentatively.

"Sorry. We're all out of sugar," the admiral apologizes. "Would artificial sweetener be all right?" I smile and nod. Gary opens a storage unit to his right. It has a built-in microwave and Gary heats up water and makes tea for both of us. The admiral serves my cup in what looks like a metal thimble—still huge in my hands—and adds a pinch of sweetener. Perfect.

I plan to fill the admiral in on the basics of what happened on Earth while he and his kin were gone. It's going to be mostly the school stuff I learned. But at least our space visitor will get the fundamentals. When I offer to share the story as I know it, Gary is delighted and waves off my concerns. I sip at my bucket of tea, and start.

"The disastrous effects of global warming began in earnest by the mid-twenty first century, decades before any serious consideration was given to helping the troubled planet." Gary nods and listens. "No nation ever responded wholeheartedly to try and prevent the climate change being generated, and as such, every country faced hotter seasons, melting glaciers, and rising sea levels.

"By the end of the twenty-second century, however, a superheated Earth had largely killed all the life in the world's oceans, and turned huge amounts of the world's farmlands into desert. There was mass starvation as the stunted produce was all that could be produced in the world's few remaining fields.

"Even as the trumpet of the Apocalypse was about to sound, the United States—still powerful and rich because it possessed over eighty percent of the Earth's surviving agriculture—began massive preparations to send people and technologies to Mars to create a habitat for American emigrants to the Red Planet. Almost a quarter of a million settlers eventually left for the Lewis and Clark Colony founded and filled with American space pioneers."

I pause and take a sip of my tea. I know that Gary is hearing stuff that he already knows. But he is a polite listener and probably figures that at some point I'll get around to explaining why Martians are still six feet tall whereas Earthlings only reach six inches. I take a couple of sips of the tea and go on.

"Even as America was sending pioneers to Mars, the European Union appealed to the nations of the world to relinquish their governing powers to the United Nations in a final worldwide effort to save the planet. The idea was stoked by the fact that most of the world's population had died and commerce had all but failed. The requirements to sustain the remaining folks were modest, and many governments believed that new safeguards protecting the planet from mankind's lawless waste could at last be enacted. Further, there was great hope that the exhausted Earth might very well regenerate itself as it had after past extinction events.

"The US refused to participate at first. But after the Middle East, Asia, and most of Africa followed Europe's example, the United States gave in. After almost five hundred years of freedom, America declared an end to its status as an independent nation. Giving up its isolation, America united with virtually every other country accepting the global rule of the United Nations.

"Old allegiances and bitter histories came to the forefront of US politics and the United States experienced a total break-up of its historic Union. Fourteen new nations rose in the place of

TALL WAR

the old republic, with only four states pledging themselves to a continued collaboration as the United States.

"Empowered by the remaining wealth and energy of the nations of the world, the United Nations focused on preserving whatever small portion of the global ecology it could save, while simultaneously utilizing advanced biological and genetic technologies to launch a multi-generational project to reduce mankind's physical size from six feet to six inches tall. They called it Downsizing. As you can see, it worked."

Gary looks astonished.

"Tell me more," is all he can say.

"With a several-hundred-year timeline for its unprecedented attempt at reinventing humanity's size and controlling its masses," I continue, "the UN allowed Earth's already greatly diminished population of one and a half billion people to decline to a constant population of some two million people. It remains at that number today.

"The planet rebounded as hoped, and human activity was confined mostly to raising crops and livestock. Medical technologies were preserved and advanced with significant progress in disease control, the enhancement of personal health and wellness through genetic engineering, and the creation of new everyday conveniences such as netacts—internet lenses in the eyes—and RediMedi prescriptive suits." Also, I think to myself, some great sex drugs, none of which I mention to Friedman.

"Whoa," Gary gasps when I finish. "You've been on an almost unimaginable journey. Up until now I thought our Mars adventure had been a real challenge. But you folks saved the entire planet." The admiral shakes his head at the wonder of it. "Absolutely amazing," he says. "Would it be okay if I asked some questions?"

"Sure," I answer and stand up to stretch. My butt's asleep. Zippo'd.

"You said that the United States yielded its governing powers to the United Nations," Gary begins. "Does that mean it disbanded its armed forces?"

Friedman's first question stops me dead in my tracks. I guess that his being in the military and all would give rise to him asking for that kind of information, but I have to admit that his choice of that subject unnerves me. I just told him about the brave new world we live in and he wants to know if America got rid of its soldiers.

"Yes, that's what it means," I answer, as civil as I can make my voice sound.

"Then where did the troops outside come from?" the admiral asks. "And if they are UN troops, what is their chain of command? Is the UN free to occupy American soil or does it need permission from Washington?"

Soldier or not, Friedman is starting to piss me off. Who cares where the soldiers come from? But before I can get ornery and make an ass of myself, General Wainwright throws up some data on my netacts and suggests that I use it. I do.

"United Nations' troops are professional volunteers from all the nations of the Earth," I tell the admiral. "You might find it interesting that men and women commit to a thirty-year career. Their pay and benefits continue after retirement, at which time they also receive a home in the city or town of their choosing. Or if they prefer, a working farm wherever they wish to live."

"Are the soldiers genetically enhanced?" Friedman asks.

"*All* humans are genetically designed and produced under UN population and occupation quotas," I read off Wainwright's

TALL WAR

crib screen. "Soldiers, however, are citizens who opt to bypass their assigned careers in favor of service in the military. Time has proven that volunteers make the best soldiers."

"Sort of like husbands," Gary offers and chuckles at his own joke. "How often are soldiers in combat situations?"

"Never," I answer on my own. "Well, not for the past couple of hundred years anyway."

"Because there are no wars?"

"Because there are no wars."

"But there were wars earlier?" he asks.

"Yes. There were two global Downsizing wars, each lasting several decades."

"Well, I have to admit I'm not surprised," Gary says. "There must have been nations who weren't willing to go quietly into *that* good night."

"Such as?" I ask, having no idea what the heck he is talking about.

The admiral picks up the challenge with gusto.

"First of all, I'd guess that some countries with significant military capabilities defied the UN's edict to have their armies stand down. There was probably also pushback from the world's richest corporations. Super states accountable to no one really. Unwilling to surrender control of their monopolies on food, water, or energy."

Gary pauses and thinks for a moment.

"There were also probably some serious one-off conflicts. Perhaps with the Roman Catholic Church. Or maybe with some Islamic nations if they got their act together. Almost certainly there would have been a serious confrontation with the Cosa Nostra, an invisible empire dragged into the light of day by

Downsizing. Any one of these challenges to United Nations' control could have spiraled into wars that would have taken longer to win than anybody ever would have expected."

Friedman stops and studies my face.

"How'd I do?" he asks.

"You pretty much nailed everything," I tell him, impressed by how quickly and how thoroughly he detailed exactly the kinds of confrontations the Downsizing generations experienced. "There were two world wars and dozens of limited—but bloody—engagements against special interest groups. Downsizing won in the end, but not without a price."

"And it's been a couple of hundred years since all this happened?" Friedman asks.

"Yes."

"That's a long time," Gary muses. "So, the full-size humans—"

"The *Originals*," I correct him. "Big O."

"So, the Originals have been gone for—" Gary pauses and waits for me to finish.

"Almost four hundred years," I fill in for him.

Gary wrinkles his forehead at that. Then frowns more deeply as the significance of that number works its way through his filters.

"What happened to their cities, and their machines, and everything else they built?" Gary looks anxious.

Who cares, I think. With the Originals gone, who'd want the stuff they left behind? None of it was really valuable or usable. Just damned big. Which Final is going to pull on a pair of 34 X 34 jeans? And I'd love to see the Final girl who could fill a 36DD bra.

"Everything is gone," I tell him. "Torn down, fallen apart, hauled away, recycled. A few things were so big that they were

TALL WAR

left alone. The Pyramids and the Great Wall. The Eiffel Tower and the Empire State Building."

"What about Fenway Park?" Gary asks, a look of hope on his face. He jumps up and opens a cupboard over the work station. He reaches in and pulls out an old-fashioned baseball hat with a big red *B* stitched on front. He puts it on, then looks at me and waits.

"Don't know about Fenway Park," I tell him. Friedman's shoulders droop.

"What was it?" I ask.

"A baseball stadium in Boston," he answers. "Home of the Red Sox."

"Baseball hasn't been played in Boston for hundreds of years," I tell him.

"Really?" Gary says, a bleak look on his face. In a moment he perks up again, hope flooding back. "What about hockey?"

CHAPTER 15

Gary Friedman learns to his dismay that all of Boston's once-great sports teams are gone. No Red Sox. No Bruins. And no Celtics. His funk is profound until he realizes that New York's Yankees, Rangers, and Knicks are also as extinct as dinosaurs. He makes a spectacular recovery.

"All right," he says. "So, people are smaller now and apparently a lot less interested in sports. What about the flora and fauna?" His words fly past me without stopping. Like bees with their navigation systems down. Gary watches me. I must look like I just got poleaxed. "Plants and animals?" he tries.

"Everything else on the planet was left unchanged," I tell him, relieved that he's asking about something I know. Oh, crap. I realize that I just tossed Gary the whole enchilada. Small people and monster animals. "I milk cows that are ten times taller than me," I say. "And three hundred times heavier." Might as well totally fess up.

Gary stares at me. I figure he is trying to imagine how in the world a tiny guy like me can milk giant cows. The commander

TALL WAR

shows his class though by not asking me. Instead, he puts me at ease with his humor.

"That makes me *really* think about a barbeque now," he says. He rubs his hands together like he's ready to do whatever it takes to make that happen right now.

I grin.

Gary laughs at his own goofiness and explains.

"I can't tell you how many old American television shows I watched as a kid whose families were having a backyard barbeque. Everyone chowing down on great, big, juicy steaks. I mean, before puberty, grilled steaks were the only things I ever fantasized about." Suddenly the admiral's face darkens. "I've never had meat, Ben," he says obviously worried. "Will that cause me any problems? I mean, like dairy?"

"It shouldn't," I reassure him. "I've never heard of meat intolerance if there even is such a thing."

The skipper looks relieved.

"Hello?" someone calls from outside the spacecraft's hatch.

Friedman puts his hand down on the table. I step on. He climbs the ladder to the hatch. He steps out of the capsule onto the catwalk. Another stack of wooden crates has been delivered. Undoubtedly the vegetables Cooley Firewall promised. General Wainwright is standing next to the boxes. He salutes Gary, smiling happily.

"Admiral Friedman," he says. "You can't say the people of Earth don't love you."

Gary stands in the hatch grinning.

"Excuse me, sir," a voice interrupts from inside the capsule. Gary and I both look down.

A dark-haired Original man with a trim, black moustache is looking back. It is the third and final Martian astronaut. Malcolm Saint Jean.

"Yes, Mal?" Gary responds to his crewman.

"The waste evac is not functioning."

I grimace as my nose confirms the spaceman's report. Has this guy been trying the dairy?

"For God's sake," Friedman complains. "Go shut the door."

"I didn't leave it open, sir," Saint Jean responds and turns back to look. Rigging Nash's two security fems suddenly race out of the malfunctioning service unit.

"Who the hell are they?" Saint Jean cries. He never gets an answer. An explosion inside the bathroom hurls countless metal and plastic fragments into his body and blows Gary and me right off the catwalk. Friedman falls onto the ground below. I am thrown into the Potomac. I gasp for air and claw the muddy riverbank like a mad man.

I am dragged away by the river's current. My RediMedi buoys me and I manage to look back at the capsule. Flames are shooting out of the open hatch. Then there is a second blast—even larger than the first—which literally tears the spaceship apart. Fiery pieces of metal shoot into the air like skyrockets. I dive below the water as red-hot debris plunges into the river all around me.

My suit pulls me back to the surface. Smoke is pouring out of what's left of the bottom of the space capsule. Its top and mid-section are completely gone. I can't see Friedman. Then I can't see anything at all as the river carries me away.

Suddenly I feel lightheaded. I can't feel any wounds. But that doesn't mean there aren't any. I check as much of my suit as I can to see if it is ripped or damaged. I can't find anything, and

TALL WAR

I am beginning to feel hazy. Curiously detached from what is happening. I think my suit has doped me for trauma and shock. *Or* I've lost so much blood that my RediMedi has opted to dope me with a farewell mega-morphine dose supplied by well-meaning Hospice doctors. God damn those do-gooders.

Then my nerves ignite and I feel excruciating pain in my right thigh. Broken bone? Torn muscle? This time I can tell that my RediMedi has dosed me for pain, and has given me such a wallop that I start to black out. Better than bleeding to death, I guess. Mostly out of it now. Or drowning. Or whatever. God bless those do-gooders.

CHAPTER 16

I regain consciousness. Strange to say I'm not dead. My RediMedi suit has kept me afloat. The pain killer and sedative have worn off, however, and I am now scared shitless. Not about any life-threatening injuries I might have. I'm afraid of the Potomac and what's in it. The river is churning with migrating sockeye, thrashing and bashing, and along the riverbanks giant catfish lurk in mudholes poaching luckless swimmers like the Bromdingnagians they truly are. They snagged a well-known senator once. While it didn't seem to affect the course of Congress very much, I thought it was a terrible way to go.

I can't connect with Geness. I try my netacts over and over hoping to reach her. Nothing. No connection. Nada. I wonder if my lenses are down. Or damaged. Or if there's just no signal. I keep trying until I am shoved underwater by a mass of salmon fighting their way upstream. I kick wildly against their giant silver bodies. They push past me with their big saucer eyes, giving me no more than a moment's glance.

TALL WAR

After a while, the Potomac begins to widen. By then I figure that I've been in the water for about four hours. Sooner or later the river is going to dump me into Chesapeake Bay. I try my netacts again and again. Nothing. I wonder if I can somehow get my RediMedi suit to signal my location. I know I was hurt earlier, but apparently the RediMedi dealt with it and did not need to signal for aid. While I am grateful for its efficiency, the fact is that my know-it-all suit can't possibly grasp what deep shit I'm in.

So, I float and feel sorry for myself, watching the river grow wider and wider. Then I realize that I've already washed into Chesapeake Bay. The wind is up and little snot whitecaps slap me in the face. The water tastes salty. I hear engine noise and spot two motorboats racing straight at me.

I hadn't considered death by speedboat. But here it is. Then I hear the unmistakable *wop-wop-wop* of a search-and-rescue helicopter approaching. Red Cross? Coast Guard? I see it, flying low enough to be looking for the president's missing husband.

The MSS John F Kennedy's *landing capsule* Jon Jon *has been blown up by saboteurs and its crew killed. We are searching for an American citizen who was visiting the spacers when the capsule was destroyed. He is unaccounted for and is believed to have been thrown into the Potomac by the twin blasts that demolished the Martian spaceship. By now the river may have carried him as far as Chesapeake Bay, and that is where we are searching. And hold on, folks, there he is!*

I wave my arms and scream. The boats are only yards away from running me over. I see them, but they sure as hell don't see me. I look up at the helicopter one last second. Then I suck in the biggest breath of air I can and push myself under water. I feel the vibration of the outboard motors churning above me. The roar is deafening even under water. The moment they pass I shoot for the surface. The helicopter has passed as well. I tell myself that it has to come this way again. Please, please.

The current takes me farther out into the bay. At some point the Chesapeake will stop being a bay and start being an ocean. My hands are numb, and my feet, too. Not as much as my hands though since I'm still wearing my boots. I try my netacts again. No response. But for the first time since I was flung into the Potomac I am able bring up my RediMedi files. I scan a list of my suit's med doses and authorize an injection of 1,200 milligrams of caffeine. That's like four mugs of coffee. In moments I am feeling awake, alert, and despite my circumstances, confident.

I shoot myself with caffeine another time as the afternoon passes. And just before dusk I try a third time, but my suit refuses. I am furious. It's not like I'm asking for heroin. Asshole programming. I keep trying. I don't know how hypothermia works, or how long it takes, but I can feel weariness begin to overtake me. I'm going to die in the dark. In the water. Never saw that coming. The one time I should have read my horoscope.

Ow! Something in the water just bit me in the back. It hurt like a son of a bitch. The good news is that I must not be totally frozen yet. I brace for another chomp, but instead a turtle pops his head up right in front of me. It's not all that big, but it's got an ornery-looking beak and I've already felt what it can do. The turtle eyes me for a moment. Maybe trying to figure out what I'm doing out here. It has intelligent eyes. The kind of eyes that can assess the danger I'm in and give me a ride back to civilization. Or maybe it's simply running through recipes for human.

TALL WAR

The turtle opens his beak and seizes me by the torso. My arms and legs dangle numb and useless. Then the turtle clenches his jaws tight and swims for the distant shore. Chesapeake take-out. In minutes it crawls onto the rocky beach. It stops and looks up. A giant Original human is looking down. It reaches for a big rock and hits the turtle on the head. The turtle is done for, and the huge person reaches down and takes me gently out of the dead beast's mouth. I look at my rescuer. She is wearing a blue flight suit. I recognize who it is.

"Hello," Spacer Susan Talbot says, holding me up to her face. "I wasn't sure you were still alive, little man." She touches my hands and my face. "You're cold as ice. I don't think we have much time to spare."

Talbot turns and carries me into the woods. Why is she *here*? How did she survive the capsule's destruction? And how in the world did she see me just now? She puts me down and quickly piles some fallen leaves and dry twigs together. Then she pulls out a Zippo like the one Gary had and starts a fire. Talbot kneels by me and speaks urgently.

"You have to take off your wet clothes or you'll freeze, fire or not."

"I can't move my arms," I tell her.

She can't hear me. Talbot puts her ear close to my face.

"I can't move," I say louder.

"I'll help," she says.

The astronaut quickly removes my boots. Then she unzips and pulls down my suit. I lay helpless as she wraps some kind of microfiber cloth around me, which instantly starts to make me feel warmer. Talbot positions me just close enough to the fire for me to absorb its heat without getting fried.

I get drowsy as the fire's heat begins to enter my numb body. Talbot gets up and cuts some branches from a nearby tree. Then she fashions them into some sort of makeshift rack over the fire. I try to figure out what she's doing, but I can't keep my eyes open. I don't know how long I'm out, but when I wake, it's dark and Talbot has hung some kind of pot on her cooking apparatus.

"What's that?" I ask. "Hanging over the fire."

"Say again?" she responds and leans closer.

"What's that pot hanging over the fire?" I ask louder.

"It's not a pot," she says. "It's a shell. I hope you like turtle."

CHAPTER 17

"I know who you are," I tell Susan Talbot. "I was at the landing site when you first opened the hatch."

"You heard me speak?" she asks.

"Yes. Later on, I met Admiral Friedman. We were bringing fresh food on board before the bomb went off."

"Then I know who you are, too," Talbot says. "You're Benedict Katz."

"Ben is fine."

"So is Susan."

"You saved my life," I tell her.

"Saved you *and* made you supper," she says.

I get my first smell of turtle wafting through the air.

"How did you get way down here?" I ask.

"I was sleeping when the first explosion ripped open the space capsule. I should have been killed. But somehow, I wound up in the river."

"That same explosion blew Admiral Friedman and me off

the catwalk connected to the ship," I tell Susan. "I saw him fall to the ground. I landed in the river. Like you."

Susan nods.

"That's the last time you saw him?"

I nod.

"We had talked awhile before everything happened. You were sleeping."

"Gary staggered our sleep rotations so that at any given time two crew members would be on duty in case of a crisis," she explains.

"Like what?"

"Like having the space capsule blown up."

"I'm sorry," I tell her.

Susan's face turns grim and she doesn't respond. If I were her, I don't think I would be in a mood to be forgiving anybody just yet.

"When Gary said we had to stay prepared for any kind of confrontation," Talbot continues after a few moments, "I have to admit I had trouble believing him. Everyone seemed friendly. And we were back in America, for God's sake. *Home.*" Susan pauses and frowns. "But he was right. Your government blew up our ship."

"No," I protest. "It didn't. There were spies on your ship and they were the ones who blew it up. Friedman, Saint Jean, and I all saw them running toward the hatch just before the explosion."

Talbot narrows her eyes almost to slits and stares at me.

"*Whose* spies?" she asks suddenly suspicious. "And how do you know they were responsible for the explosions?"

"To be honest, I don't really know that they were. However, I noticed that one of the politicians in our party, Rigging Nash,

TALL WAR

was accompanied by a pair of bodyguards who proceeded to disappear. I didn't know where they had gone, but I began to suspect that they may have been brought specifically to spy inside your spaceship."

Talbot studies my face. Her expression is not exactly an accusation, but she's obviously upset that I didn't tell the space travelers about my suspicions. She finally looks away, letting it go for now. She adds some branches to the fire. Then she looks at me. Her face is tender now.

"How are you?" she asks. "Warming up?"

"Well, I actually am, thank you for asking. It's nothing short of a miracle that you found me."

"I let the current take me down river away from the destruction," Talbot explains. "I was afraid that whoever had blown up the *Jon Jon* would try and exterminate all of us."

I am creeped out by Susan's choice of words. I am also creeped out by her fear that whoever blew up the Originals' space capsule would be intent on wiping them out. It's painfully obvious to me that Rigging Nash and his toadies arranged to have those bombs placed on the *Jon Jon*. But who, or what, was behind the cowardly act is still a mystery.

Whoever is responsible, I feel more guilty than ever about the dead spacemen because I kept my mouth shut when I knew from Wilson's intercepted transmissions that the ninja twins were indeed on board the capsule. Susan has been telling the story of her escape, but I haven't been listening. I tune back in.

"And that's how I wound up all the way down river. When I saw that it had emptied into the ocean, I swam to shore, dried out in the sun, and hid myself in the woods waiting for dark. At dusk I spotted the turtle climbing up onto the shore with you in its mouth. I sure as hell wasn't going to let some little green shithead eat a human. I whacked it with a big rock and that was that."

"I remember. You saved my life."

Susan smiles—the first time she has done so since she rescued me—then gets up and takes the turtle shell off of her homemade cooking rack. I try to bring my netacts online again. They're still screwed up. Or maybe, I think darkly, there's nothing wrong with them at all, and someone is blocking my internet access.

I frown, pissed off and scared again. But is it, in fact, a possibility? I have to believe so. There's no reason my netacts shouldn't work. Yet they don't. I try to pull up my RediMedi menu again. The screen tells me that my suit is inactive. What? I look at my bare arms and legs and remember that Talbot took it off.

"Where is my suit?" I call to her trying not to panic.

"Drying," she says. "I'll check on it." She retrieves the suit from the edge of the fire and hands it to me. "Good as new," she says.

God, I hope so. Susan goes back to preparing supper and gives me some privacy. I pull my suit on and zip it up. Feels okay. I check my lenses. *Connection established* the RediMedi tells me. Let's check it out. I request a dose of adrenaline. The suit collar kisses the back of my neck. Oh. Whoa. Good as new for sure.

"Susan?" I call.

She looks at me.

"I think we need to leave here. If it was Rigging Nash's agents who blew up your ship, then he's had them hunting for you ever since your body didn't turn up in the wreckage. I don't know if Nash is acting on his own, or has orders. But I can guarantee that you will be safe in Washington, the US capital near where your spaceship landed in the Potomac."

TALL WAR

"Who is Rigging Nash?" Susan asks.

"He is America's ambassador to the United Nations, a body that rules all the remaining national governments on Earth. And he is against the American government's support for the Martian visit. He has been from the beginning. If he did arrange for the explosives to be taken on board the capsule, he could have acted on his own or be secretly in cahoots with anyone."

"Cahoots?" Susan repeats. She looks puzzled.

"It means a secret partnership that's up to no good."

"Not the United Nations?"

"God, I hope not. If the world government is behind the plot then we're all boned."

Susan's face looks blank.

"In trouble," I reply, declining to reveal the intended crudeness of the expression.

"Like being fucked?" Susan asks.

I grin.

"Yeah, something like that. The point is the pressure is on and we need a plan."

Talbot gets it.

"For the six-foot woman and the six-inch man."

I nod.

"That would be the only plan I care about."

CHAPTER 18

Susan brings me a few bits of turtle on a leaf. She sets it down on the ground in front of me. I stare at the chunks of meat. I've never had turtle before. And given how it looks—dull white with flecks of green skin on some of the pieces—I haven't missed anything. There is no question, however, that I'll eat it. I'm starved. Plus, I still haven't gotten over the fact that the bastard reptile had counted on doing the same to me. I put a piece in my mouth and chew. Tastes like a cheap cut of beef.

"What do you think?" Susan asks.

"Tastes kind of like beef."

"I've never had that," she replies. "But then, I've never had turtle, either, until two minutes ago."

"I know. Gary said there wasn't any meat on Mars."

"Well," Susan murmurs, "that's not entirely true. Not that he ever would have had any. Other folks though…" she lets her voice trail off.

"What about you?" I ask her, instantly wishing that I hadn't. I realize there can only be one kind of meat on Mars and I'm pretty sure that it's not turtle.

"Me?" Susan shivers just thinking about it. "Never."

"So, how do *you* like the turtle?"

Susan puts another piece in her mouth and chews carefully.

"Hard to tell," she says. "It doesn't taste like anything I've ever had. A little sour. Some kind of savory under taste. Might be good in a stew. Or with some gravy." Susan looks at me and asks a question of her own. "Does it ever bother you to eat something that lived, and breathed, and walked around?"

"No," I answer. "It isn't doing any of those things when I eat it."

Susan laughs.

"Dumb question, eh?" she asks embarrassed.

"No. Does it bother *you* that you're eating an animal?" I ask.

"Are you kidding? I bashed its head in if you recall."

"That doesn't bother me either."

Susan laughs. And man did she bash its head in. She whacked that turtle's head so hard crap came out the back and I came out the front.

"How long did you spend with Gary?" Susan asks me while we both eat.

"Only a couple of hours," I reply.

"What did you think of him?" Talbot's trying to be nonchalant, but it's obvious that she really wants to hear my impressions. Was she involved with him? A few months short of a year on a spaceship together seems plenty long enough to fall for someone as smooth and handsome as Admiral Gary Friedman.

"You know, I liked him right away," I tell her honestly. "He seemed genuinely nice. Someone you could look up to."

"He was that," Susan says quietly. "He always was." She tears up. Some things apparently don't change. Big or small. I let Susan have her moment, averting my eyes and staring into the forest that surrounds us. There isn't a glimmer of light. I hear an owl in the trees. It gives me the creeps that I can't see it. I know it can see me.

What other kinds of wild things might be lurking? The decision to shrink people and leave animals full-size added enormous risk to even the most routine outdoor activities. Hiking in the forest. Camping by a lake. Even taking a Sunday picnic if you went farther than your own backyard.

I can't help imagining how vulnerable I'd be here in the woods if Susan weren't with me. I scootch closer to the fire and watch the flames. Suddenly I feel lonely for Geness. Many a night we snuggled in quilts in front of the fireplace at the farmhouse. Now she probably thinks I'm dead.

"Are you thinking of your wife?" Susan asks.

I look at her. She wipes away the last of her tears.

"You looked sad," she says by way of explanation.

I nod.

"I was thinking of how my wife and I would cuddle in front of our fireplace."

Susan nods. I wait for more tears. But there aren't any.

"Can I ask you something?" I say.

Susan looks at me.

"Were you and Gary together?"

"Only as crew members," she answers. "Gary and Malcolm were life partners."

Didn't see that coming. Built female sitting it out while the boys boink each other. I let that sink in. Then I realize that Gary watched his soulmate die in the capsule blast. After backing up the toilet on the spaceship with his last bowel movement. Saint Jean's exit was packed with more metaphors than I can handle right now. I'll think about it later.

"Do you have someone special back on Mars?" I ask Talbot.

"No, I don't," Susan answers. "There aren't enough to go around."

Not enough men? Or not enough partners? Of for that matter, not enough women? Not everyone on Earth gets a partner, but it has nothing to do with availability. Finals are produced in labs with our fates pretty much planned out. Parents are assigned for our childhood years. Then we're trained for a specific career. Sometimes were assigned to a spouse. And on very rare occasions approved to bear a child. Exceptions can occur. Love affairs. Divorces. Early deaths. Blah, blah, blah. The best laid plans of government authorities can still go astray when you figure in a sprinkling of free will that no amount of genetic manipulation has been able to weed out.

"Could I ask you some more questions about your home?" I ask.

"Yes," she responds. "Then I get to ask you some, Ken."

"Ben," I correct her.

"I know," Susan chuckles. "I'm teasing."

I am surprised, but happy, to see that there's some girl left in the woman.

She begins.

"On Mars little girls play with dolls that look like the ones brought from Earth by the earliest settlers. One is named Barbie. Another is her boyfriend Ken. He looks a lot like you. Thick hair. Brown eyes. Body to die for."

I blush. I forgot that Talbot saw me naked.

"You're pretty, ah, well-built," she says, and smiles shyly.

"You mean for a little guy," I reply.

"For any guy," Susan says. "Made *me* wet."

Now I flush fiery hot. I decide to take it like a man.

"What are you talking about?" I ask.

"I think you know," Susan tells me and smiles again. This time a bit flirty. "You're a good-looking guy, Ben. Gives a girl thoughts."

I blush again. I'm not sure if Susan is just yanking my chain, but I have to admit that she's really making me embarrassed. She notices how obvious my discomfort has become and grins.

"So why aren't there enough partners on Mars?" I ask.

Susan smiles again, and answers.

"The Colony population began to grow as soon as hydroponic food production and solar energy yields allowed for it. A hundred years after the settlement's founding, more than a million and a half people lived on Mars. It took dozens of decades for exploding food and energy production levels to max out, and by then the population was close to three million. To keep things balanced, rules were enacted to regulate pregnancies and live births in order to stabilize Mars' population at a constant three million people."

"Did anyone ever mention returning to Earth?"

Susan frowns, puzzled.

"Why would you ask that?"

I shrug. It just seems that when controls get put in place there's always someone who thinks that there must be greener pastures somewhere else. The fact was, the Earth was indeed greener at that point. But how would the Martians have known that?

TALL WAR

"No one on Mars ever talked about going back," Susan continues. "There was no point. The United Nations forbid repatriation, and just before all communications between the two planets were officially blacked out by the UN in 2272 we were told that all of Earth's military and commercial space vehicles had been grounded and dismantled."

"Slowed you down getting back here."

"Yes," Susan agrees. "By about five centuries. But then some forty years ago we began to construct nuclear plants. It was inevitable that *that* activity would re-open the door to space travel."

"But why did you choose archaic Thrusters and Capsules technologies?" I ask, repeating the name of my favorite TV show about that era. "Why didn't you build more advanced, reusable spacecrafts? Space shuttles with round-trip capabilities?"

"To what purpose?" Susan responds. "Our only goal in coming back here was to see if anything, or anyone, had survived."

"So, you landed in a capsule with no way back off the planet? Pretty brave."

Susan shrugs.

"Or pretty stupid," she comments.

"And why you? Why were you picked for this mission? And what about Gary and Malcolm?"

"Gary came because he had spent his entire life hoping to see what had happened to the Earth. He talked about it. He trained for it. He campaigned endlessly to be one of the people designated to return here. Malcolm came because he grew up exactly the same way. Harboring the same hope in his heart. Spending his life working out that passion. He and Gary were both accepted into the program, and while they trained their friendship grew to the point where they made a commitment to be life partners." Susan pauses. Then she looks me in the eye. "And I came along because I was Gary's lover."

CHAPTER 19

"How old are you, Ben?" Susan asks before I can question her about the bombshell she just dumped in my lap.

"Twenty-seven."

"I'm thirty-one."

"Is that young or old on Mars?"

"Extremely young," Susan answers. "The average colonist lives for about a hundred and fifty years."

"A hundred and fifty years?" I yelp.

Susan stares at me.

"That surprises you?"

"I'd say so," I declare. "Down here no one lasts much past sixty."

Susan frowns as though I just slapped her one.

"You guys kill each other off?"

"No," I reply offended at the suggestion. "People get old. They die."

"Of what?" Susan asks.

"Heart attacks. Strokes. Diabetes. Cancer. Those sorts of things."

"I don't recognize any of them," Talbot replies. "When do people on Earth start to show signs of aging?"

"Around forty or so. Men and women are usually young and healthy up to that point. After that there is a slow physical decline through the fifties. Then old. Or dead."

"On Mars, people take synthetic growth hormones to maintain their immune systems," Susan says. "In *their* fifties they begin replacing body parts with 3D printed duplicates. Better than duplicates actually, as they are manufactured from new stem cells. You can even get a replacement brain if you have the money. After a person reaches one hundred and twenty, he or she may elect voluntary euthanasia."

"They can choose to be put down?"

"That's a little blunt. But yes."

"Here you work till you drop."

"What do you do, Ben?"

"I run a dairy farm."

"Cows?"

"I have ten. I milk them twice a day." I stop for a moment. "When I'm home." I can hear the sadness in my own voice. I didn't do it on purpose. Just sort of crept in from my heart, I guess.

"And you said you were married," Susan continues. "Does your wife work, too?"

Before I can answer, Susan suddenly stands. She quickly puts a finger to her lips and stamps out the fire. She motions for me to follow and hurries silently into the woods. I run as fast as I can to keep up with her. She stops behind a big tree and pulls some kind of pistol out of a holster. She stands silently and we both wait. It isn't long before I see what alarmed her. A group of Finals converge on the remains of our fire. There are four of them.

"He's gone," a female says.

"What was your first clue?" a male sneers in response.

"The fire is still—"

"Shut up."

Hells bells. I am sure that pissed-off asshole is Rigging Nash's minion Adrian Modigliarty.

"He's still close," another man says. "The GPS is stationary and the signal is strong."

"Someone hand me a light," Modigliarty orders.

In a moment he has a flashlight and starts kicking the fire until the embers burst into flame again. I can see his face and I can see the man he was talking to. A meaty specimen with bodybuilder muscles. The other two Finals are females. I'm pretty sure they're the same agents who blew up Talbot's space capsule.

"I'm going to sit down," Adrian says. He does, close to the fire. The man with him is wearing a silver RediMedi, a soldier's uniform. He's either UN military or a mercenary. Modigliarty and both of the fems have on black suits. Top civilian stuff. All four of them are wearing utility belts with holsters for pistols and lasers. Everyday citizens are not allowed to have those. So, of course, only criminals do. The rednecks were right. God bless their suspicious little minds.

"Sir, why don't you head back to the boat?" Modigliarty's companion asks. "The gals can see you there safely and I'll find Katz on my own."

"You couldn't find him in the daylight," Adrian snaps at him. "You sure as hell aren't going to find him in the dark."

"But I know he's here," the man objects. "I have him on the tracker, which means he's a dead man. Just a matter of when."

"Stop talking like some shithead on a TV show," Modigliarty growls.

"Just telling you how I see it," the man insists.

"It's dark, fuck for brains. You can't see anything. All right?" Modigliarty snarls.

This time the man doesn't respond. He and the females sit down by the fire. Away from Modigliarty. He starts a conversation with someone on his netacts. Probably Rigging Nash. Telling him that I'm in the crosshairs.

I move closer to Susan. I step on a twig that snaps loudly.

"It's Katz!" Modigliarty shouts. "Shoot him!" Blue targeting lasers cut through the trees surrounding me. I take off into the woods snapping stuff like a maniac. I run deep into the forest and hide under a pile of leaves for a long time after the blue lasers stop. Then I slowly circle back until I can see the fire from the other side of the woods. Modigliarty and his goons are still standing there, looking at where I fled into the woods.

Suddenly the man next to Modigliarty cries out and crumples to the ground. Adrian stares at him in amazement. Then one of the females screams in agony and sinks to her knees. She lifts her hands and grabs her head. In a moment she falls on her face. Even as she does her companion cries out and collapses. Only Modigliarty is left standing.

Susan Talbot steps out of the woods with her pistol trained on him. Adrian hesitates, and then—in what is probably the stupidest decision of his life—he attempts to raise his laser gun at her. Susan kicks her foot and both he and his pistol go flying. Modigliarty hollers in pain. Lying on the ground he holds his hand and looks up at the giant woman towering over him. I leave the cover of the woods and run over to where Susan has Modigliarty cornered.

"I don't have an issue with you!" he cries sitting up.

"You tried to shoot me," Susan responds, pissed. "Or doesn't that count?"

"It was self-defense!" Modigliarty cries. "You shot my team!"

Adrian stands slowly. He is cradling a bleeding hand. He stares up at Talbot. "I repeat. I don't have any issues with you," he says defiantly.

"But *she* might have an issue with you, Adrian," I shout and run into the clearing. "Your boss sent your two female accomplices into the moored spaceship to kill her and everyone in it."

Modigliarty looks like he could burst.

"You lie!" he screams.

"No way. I saw your agents running across the capsule floor just before it blew. So did astronauts Malcolm Saint Jean *and* Gary Friedman. So, where were you? Hiding nearby to give the order to destroy the capsule and kill the astronauts?"

Adrian's face is screwed into a furious mask, but he controls himself. Which is smart in that all of his other companions have been shot down and he is defenseless before Talbot and her pistol.

"Who are you taking orders from?" I demand.

"Who do you think?" Modigliarty snaps. He holds himself rigid, clasping his injured hand.

"Well, it's not the United Nations," I tell him stepping closer. "Murdering Admiral Friedman and his crew was hardly the diplomatic solution one would expect of the world government."

"It *was* the United Nations!" Adrian snaps. "After hundreds of years of creating a new human race and stabilizing the Earth, what possible good could come out of the return of selfish, devil-may-care Originals?"

I am angry at Modigliarty. But I will be furious beyond belief if it's true that the UN took the low path—the despicable path—of assassinating the humans who came from Mars. Susan sees my anger, but wants an answer to a question that I haven't even thought of.

"Why were you searching for Ben?" she asks. "And why did you order your subordinates to shoot when you thought you had found him?"

"None of your business," Modigliarty says in a flippant tone. "You were the official object of the search. But Mr. Nash ordered me to take out Katz if our efforts snagged him. He figured that both of you had survived and been swept down the river. So, it was no great surprise to find you two in the same place."

"You still haven't answered my question," Talbot repeats in a menacing tone of voice. Modigliarty does not miss her threat. And she is still holding the pistol that killed all of his team. Adrian finally speaks.

"Mr. Nash expects Geness Jones to be a significant opponent of the United Nations' decision to eliminate the Originals. He thought that by eliminating her husband it would emotionally handicap her in the debate and turmoil coming over the Security Council's decision."

"I don't understand," Susan says.

"Then you must not know that Mrs. Jones is Katz's wife and is the president of the United States in whose territory your capsule landed."

Talbot's face shows her surprise and she looks at me with deep disappointment. Modigliarty chooses that moment to carry out his prime directive. He pulls out a concealed knife and lunges at me. Talbot brings down her boot instantly and grinds him into the ground. Oh, God.

I fall to my knees and hurl my guts out.

CHAPTER 20

I slowly get to my feet. Susan lifts up her boot and looks at the bottom. She stares at the smeared remains of Adrian Modigliarty, then wipes the sole on the grass. I turn away and throw up a second time. My legs feel wobbly. I go down on my butt. The way Talbot tromped Modigliarty has really screwed me up. I put my head between my knees and take some deep breaths. After a while I stand up again and try not to look at the stain on the grass that used to be Rigging Nash's evil shadow.

I shouldn't feel so bad. But I've never seen a person crushed out of existence in a fraction of a second. The sheer brutality of Talbot's response also makes me fear her for the first time. Not only because of her strength, but also for the curious lack of conscience that allowed her to judge, condemn, and execute Adrian Modigliarty when she could have just disarmed him. It's also going to be pretty hard to get any information out of him now, too.

TALL WAR

"Well, you were right that people would be out searching for us," Susan says staring at me. "You just forgot to tell me why they'd be searching for *you*."

"I'm not important," I argue back. "They were looking for you. The Original who escaped dying in the explosions. Killing me was just Nash's little side project to fuck with Geness. And so what if you didn't know my wife was president? She didn't order the murders. And for that matter, she couldn't prevent them.

"You can be as pissed as you want because you think I kept you in the dark," I go on.

"You can stand here and pout. Or you can get us out of here before more teams show up now that they know exactly where to look."

Susan eyes me for a moment.

"Let's go," she tells me without any rebuttal, not that I've heard the last of this, I'm sure. She starts to slip her pistol back into its holster.

"Can I see your weapon?" I ask quickly. "I never heard it fire."

Susan holds out her gun for me to inspect. It is shaped like a regular pistol but the barrel is thin. Like a pencil. And solid. Also, there is a metal box behind the trigger guard instead of a laser chamber.

"It's a neutron gun," Talbot explains. "Chamber initiates a miniature thermonuclear reaction, which leaves the barrel and enters the target as a beam of neutrons. They disrupt the genetic makeup of the cells they pass through, killing organs, blood cells, everything. Causes almost instant death."

"I heard a lot of screaming."

"I didn't say it didn't hurt."

"Why didn't you just shoot Modigliarty?"

"I wanted information from him."

"Me, too."

"Sorry I had to step on him."

"Not a problem. I hope he doesn't smell up your boot."

Susan looks at me to see if I'm being a smart ass. I'm not.

She lifts her boot and checks the bottom again. She wipes it in the grass one more time.

We hike alongside the Potomac. I can hear the salmon laboring up the river in the dark. The water writhes with their efforts to swim upstream against the current. Just before dawn Susan stops and tells me, "Wait here."

She steps into the river and pulls out her neutron pistol. She aims at a churning whirlpool near the riverbank. In moments, several salmon float to the surface. Susan sorts through the fish and grabs the one she wants. She holds it up for me to see.

"Breakfast," she says.

I stare at the dead fish left floating on the water. I wonder if Talbot has any idea of how much food she's just wasted. Probably not. Though you'd think that all those years on Mars would have made her a little more frugal with resources. Humans made the mistake of being wasteful before. We don't need to make it again.

As the sun rises Susan lays down beneath a tall pitch pine. She closes her eyes after making sure I'm within reach.

"Get some sleep," she tells me.

"I will," I answer. I don't hear a reply. Then I hear Talbot's gentle breathing, followed shortly by relaxed, deep breaths. I, on the other hand, can't sleep. I am still bothered by the violence I witnessed today. I should be grateful that Talbot saved my life and that she stopped Modigliarty in his tracks. But all I can think about are his flesh and bones mashed into the ground.

TALL WAR

I also have recurring images of the two women and the man dying in agony after being shot by Talbot. I had never seen a dead person before today, and now I've witnessed the cruel and utterly painful terminations of four Finals. By an Original. A first-class killing machine who is lying next to me sleeping the sleep of the innocent. Jesus, she's good at killing. What if she is just getting started?

Haunted by those thoughts it takes me a long time to go to sleep. When I do, I dream of Gen. She is walking along the Potomac searching for me. I wave to her. She waves both of her arms and runs toward me. I hug her and tell her over and over how much I love her. She pulls my clothes off and we do it right on the grass by the river. Be it God, or the universe, or just my dick, I clutch at my dream as a sign of things to come.

CHAPTER 21

I wake up early in the afternoon. The woods are quiet. No one has been here in a very long time. Maybe never. The forest floor is thick with leaves and needles accumulated over countless decades without the presence of humankind. Kiss that goodbye. Talbot has a fire going and is cooking a salmon on her trademark rack of green branches. For a person who has cooked meat only once before in her life, she seems to have figured out the barbeque thing fast enough.

She sees that I'm awake. We don't talk. I have the blues. Maybe she does too. I miss my wife and my son. And my cows. I miss my coffee. I'd like to indulge in an anti-depressant, but my netacts lenses are still non-functional, so I cannot access the RediMedi menu for my suit. That means no caffeine either. Sooner or later, I'm going to have the mother of all headaches.

I wonder what Talbot misses. Mars? Friends and family? Does she miss Gary Friedman? She flew a zillion miles with him to come here. And she was sleeping with him. Those things gotta count for something.

Susan interrupts my thoughts.

"Do you want some salmon? It has a rich, savory flavor with a slightly sweet aftertaste." She holds out a leaf with a few morsels of salmon on it.

"Never had fish before," I tell her. "Don't like googly eyes."

"You're not eating the eyes," she says, and pushes the pieces at me.

I lift a piece of salmon up to my nose. It doesn't smell fishy. Smells like, like, I don't know.

That actually doesn't matter anyway. It's the *taste* that I'm worried about. Talbot puts the leaf on my lap. Then she sits down by the fire and eats chunk after chunk of the fish. I finally put a pinch on my tongue. Not bad. Not like turtle.

"I think you're a born meat eater," I tell Talbot as she breaks a piece of salmon into smaller bits for me.

"Think so?" she replies. "Is there such a thing as a meatatarian on this planet?"

I ponder that for a minute. Would that be a carnivore who doesn't eat vegetables? Or just someone who prefers meat if it's available? I decide it's the first. A meat eater who won't eat anything *but* meat.

"There are some of those actually," I tell Susan. "Lions and tigers and other big animals." I've never actually seen any of those except in vids. Once virtually extinct, they have all come back in dramatic numbers. So dramatic, in fact, that we now see news vids about Finals being consumed by lions or crocodiles. Meatatarians.

"I know about those," Talbot confirms. "From Earth TV. I once saw Barney at the zoo."

"Barney?" I don't know any Barneys.

"The big purple dinosaur?" Susan asks, hoping to jog the toy box part of my memory. I try to remember ever seeing a purple dinosaur while I watch Susan fill her mouth with fish. Her jaws bulge with the huge piece she just shoved in. This girl is not dainty.

"So, Barney lives in a zoo?" I ask, drawing a blank on purple dinosaurs.

"No," Susan says. "He *takes* kids to a zoo and they all dance and sing."

Dancing and singing at the zoo. With a purple dinosaur. I don't know what to say. Talbot either dreamed this up on her own or imagined it, using some non-regulated pharmaceuticals.

Susan takes my empty leaf and breaks up another hunk of salmon. She puts it down in front of me.

"What's your favorite meat?" she asks.

"Bacon," I answer without hesitation.

"Is that pig?"

"Pork," I correct her. I don't eat pig, but I do eat pork. "Pork roast. Pork chops. Pork tenderloin. Ribs, sausage, feet, and bacon."

Talbot frowns and stares at me.

"You eat the feet?"

"Of course, not. You eat the meat between the toes."

Susan stops shoving salmon in her mouth and thinks about that. Then she finishes shoving it in. Good girl. If you can think about pig's feet while you're eating something else, there isn't much that you won't stick in your mouth.

"Did you know Gary was doing some serious thinking about meat after you guys got here?" I ask.

TALL WAR

"That actually started a long time ago," Susan tells me, amused. "He fantasized forever about osso buco, bratwurst, sweetbreads, and most of all barbecued steaks."

I look at Susan.

"How'd you get so big without eating meat?"

"Same way you manage to stay so small still eating it."

It'll take a better man than me to figure that out.

"By the way," I reply. "If you start eating a lot of meat down here, you're never going to live to be a hundred and fifty."

"You mean because it's not healthy?"

"In the quantities you like, definitely not."

"I hear you. But it's more likely that somebody will shoot me in the butt first," is Talbot's philosophical comeback.

"I don't think that would be fatal."

"Not when you have a tush the size of mine. But you get my point."

"I do."

"So, what's the problem with meat?"

"The problem is with *too much* meat," I tell her. "It's got serious fat and cholesterol and sooner or later consuming big portions of it damages the blood vessels, the heart, and other organs."

"But cholesterol is a simple steroid alcohol," Susan responds. "It actually helps keep arterials healthy."

"Yeah, if you don't become a meataholic," I answer.

"Son of a bitch," Susan says and looks at the salmon still on the rack.

"Actually, fish is okay," I tell her. "And chicken, too. But beef and pork will end it all for the big eater. Sort of like a built-in autodestruct program."

Susan glances at me.

"What are you talking about?"

"The body's version of the autodestruct software built into military hardware. If a plane, or tank, or ship is captured by the enemy, the destruct mechanism is engaged and blows it up. I was surprised that your space capsule didn't have an autodestruct application."

"How do you know that?" Susan asks. Her voice is calm, but I can hear an unmistakable edge.

Shit. I blabbed. Again. I wish I could take back what I just said. But I can't. I opt to tell Talbot the truth.

"The two spies who snuck aboard *Jon Jon* hacked into its onboard computers. They radioed their findings and we intercepted them."

Susan is upset now and makes no effort to hide it.

"They compromised our computer system and you didn't tell us?" she says, her voice shrill.

"No, we didn't." I am ashamed and embarrassed. Why *didn't* we say anything? I can't even imagine what stupid reason we had for not telling the Martian crew that there were spies aboard their ship.

"What the fuck, Ben," Susan says totally pissed. "That kind of shit is inexcusable. You folks knew that there were spies on the *Jon Jon*, that they had hacked into our computers, and yet you were still goddamn surprised when they blew up our ship?" Talbot looks away disgusted. She stands up and heads into the woods.

Nice going, Mr. Congressman Volunteer. You can turn in your badge anytime.

CHAPTER 22

Susan comes back. But not for hours. She has scavenged some dead branches and throws them on the ashes of the earlier fire. She stuffs some moss and leaves under the branches and starts a new fire with her Zippo. While she was gone, I realized that my farm is pretty much a straight shot west of here. We'd have to cross the Potomac. But that's really the only obstacle. At least the only one I know about. We're about ten or twelve miles away. That's a hell of a hike for me. But I am hoping Talbot will be over her anger and carry me.

Susan sits by the fire and calls to me after a while.

"Ben? I'd feel better if I could see where you are."

I walk over.

"I'm still really upset," she warns me. "But not at you. I realized that you couldn't really do much about anything that was happening. Your *wife* is responsible. Not you."

That's actually true, though I don't like Talbot taking a shot at Geness. Unfortunately, my fair-minded spouse gave Rigging

Nash the benefit of the doubt over my objections, and in this case, she was deceived. I wonder if she and her father, Wilson, have been able to identify the members of the Security Council who gave Nash the go ahead to kill the spacemen rather than bring up their fate with the General Assembly.

It was a despotic and undemocratic decision. It was also shameful and unforgiveable. Only time will tell what the folks back on Mars will be capable of doing when they find out the despicable news of the deaths of Admiral Friedman and Malcolm Saint Jean. Susan holds out her hand to me. I climb on and she lifts me up onto her thigh.

"Are you hungry?" she asks.

"Do you have any bacon?"

Talbot grins.

"No. I found some blackberries, though. Do you like those?"

"I do."

She puts a huge blackberry down in front of me. It's about the size of a dumpster.

"Don't get a stain on my suit." Susan looks at me sternly. "I'm not kidding."

I stare at the blackberry. I have never seen a whole one before. Looks like the eye of a fly, its thousand black pupils looking at me. I buy packages of those little segments at the store when they show up once in a while. Not many Finals hunt for blackberries. I don't.

I'm not willing to compete with birds, raccoons, or deer for them. Not to mention that some of those animals would gladly trade up from a blackberry to a six-inch farmer. I pull one of the little blackberry bulbs away from the core. It is juicy, sugary, and tart. I consume the berry, bit by bit. Talbot watches me

TALL WAR

"They're called drupelets," she says.

"What is called a drupelet?" I ask.

"Those little sections that you're eating one at a time."

"Okay," I say. Drupelet. What idiot came up with that? It's a demeaning name for something wonderful. Probably the same fellow who came up with fellatio and cunnilingus. Boy. Names that really capture the pleasures of those activities.

Susan eats thirty or forty of them. Blackberries. Not drupelets. She's going to regret that in the middle of the night. We sit watching the fire for a while. Susan's concern for my welfare and survival makes me feel more and more like a hypocrite. This seems as good a time as any to confess my actual role in the loss of the capsule and Talbot's crew.

"Susan, I want to say that I'm sorry—"

"Stop," she orders sharply, and holds up her hand.

"But—"

"What's done is done," she interrupts again. "We have to survive. I can't think about anything else. Not now." Her tone is tough. But her eyes get teary. Then she begins to sob.

"This is not how we imagined it would be," she says softly. "We thought the Earth might be barren and abandoned. And that we'd probably die. What we found instead was a magnificent world. As beautiful as the day humans first walked upon it." Talbot wipes her tears away. "Only now smaller humans were walking on it. And the first thing they did was try and kill us." Susan looks at me. Her face is drawn and sad. "Why, Ben?" she asks. "What happened here while we were gone?"

I tell her. More than I ever told Gary. I tell her about Downsizing. And the wars. And the rise of the Finals who inherited the Earth only because Originals and Intermediates—and even several generations of robots—sacrificed themselves to make it happen.

"Did Gary get to hear this?" Susan asks when I am finished.

"He did," I reply. "We were talking about it just before the first explosion rocked the capsule."

"I'm glad," Talbot responds earnestly. "He always believed that somehow the Earth would have been spared. That it was waiting for us to come back again. Gary's father was very religious. So religious, in fact, that he refused to believe that God had allowed the Earth to perish. His very words. He drove the colony's effort to revitalize space travel claiming it was time for the humans on Mars to return to Earth. Gary was picked for the mission and he fulfilled his father's dream. Discovering that the planet had indeed survived, verdant and beautiful."

"What about the fact that there were still people hanging around?" I ask. Not trying to be a smart ass, but being discovered by Gary and his space crew sounds like America being *discovered* by Christopher Columbus. No one ever mentions that he ran into thirty million Caribs and North American aboriginals who'd been living there happily for tens of thousands of years. "Was that a problem for Gary?"

Susan ponders my question for a moment. Is she trying to remember Gary's reaction? Or figuring some way to sugarcoat it? I'll never forget *her* own words when she saw us gathered at the Potomac. "Where are all the big people?" Her unvarnished dismissal of the Final-size humans she encountered that day may well have mirrored Friedman's own surprise and disappointment in who he found here.

Talbot answers slowly.

"I wouldn't say Gary thought that finding people here was a problem. More like a *condition* to be dealt with."

I don't like that wording. A condition? Like a rash, or parasites?

"All right," I say, trying to sound neutral. I am convinced though that Talbot is not telling me everything. "Do you know if Gary had any directives in case you encountered any survivors on Earth?"

"He did," Susan says. "He shared with both Malcolm and me that in the event humans still populated the globe, he was to negotiate a peaceful co-existence between Earth and Mars, and secure permission for the return *over time* (Talbot's emphasis) of Martians who desired to migrate back to this world."

"And if the Earth folks resisted?" I ask. That earns me a sharp look from Talbot.

"Did you miss the fact that Gary's orders were to negotiate?" she asks irritably. "Which Gary was brilliant at. Mostly because he believed with all of his heart that anything was possible." Susan's expression darkens. "Turns out you killed him before he could try."

I flush. But instead of taking Susan's accusation like a man, I try to brush it off with a sarcastic remark.

"Well, at least the folks on the next ship will know they better have their guns handy, eh?"

Susan grimaces.

"You may not have to wait that long," she says quietly. "The mother ship we left in orbit has significant weaponry and it can be controlled from Mars. Our capsule was nothing but a big old tub meant to splash down full of friendly faces. The spaceship orbiting Earth is equipped with twenty-four missiles tipped with neutron bombs."

Talbot doesn't relate this doomsday news as a threat. She simply presents it as matter-of-fact information. The Originals on Mars sent three spacemen and enough weaponized hardware to destroy every human life on the Earth.

I swallow hard. Sweat breaks out on my forehead. My RediMedi proves it's still functional on automatic by patching me with a dose of Valium. I finally croak my freaked-out response.

"Your mother ship carries two dozen missiles?"

"Yes."

"Just in case the Earth had to be subdued before returning Martians could be fruitful and multiply?" Holy fuck. Sarcasm again. Where is that coming from all of a sudden? Some recessive British gene I carry that has decided to strut its stuff?

"Stop it," Susan demands, not amused. "No communications have been sent to Mars other than a single radio signal confirming that we landed safely."

Is that supposed to reassure me? I can't exactly construe her words as a promise that the two-dozen neutron bombs flying around over our heads won't ever be used. And I also don't really have any idea what *else* Talbot may eventually tell the Martians, which may, in the long run, be ignored since Mars controls the ship's weapon systems and can do whatever it wants, whenever it wants.

Jesus, Joseph, and Mary.

CHAPTER 23

"I'm sorry your reassurances aren't getting through to me," I honestly confess to Susan. "No matter how I look at it, I just don't understand why you brought missiles." I am emotionally gutted just *thinking* about doomsday weapons pointed at our perfect, innocent Earth. It's been almost a thousand years since madmen exploded two of those atom-splitting weapons and killed hundreds of thousands of innocent lives. And now there are *twenty-four* of them aimed at us.

"I don't think they are meant to be used," Talbot responds, trying to rationalize how two dozen weapons of mass destruction loaded onto the Martian mother ship was somehow a reasonable preparation for the journey to Earth. "They're more of a deterrent."

"A deterrent like, 'Better let us do what we want on your planet, or we'll blast you to smithereens?'" I translate for Susan. Oh, that was good, Ben, I tell myself. Can you rachet up the inflammatory language just a little more so Talbot will decide that you're not even worth talking to?

"It could have been worse, Ben," Susan responds patiently. She is still trying to help me accept a reality that I can't do anything about. "Some of the bids for a deterrent capability were submitted for plain old thermonuclear bombs."

I stare at Susan, more dumbfounded with each sentence she utters.

"Are you telling me that the Earth was almost going to be attacked by the lowest bidder?" I ask panicking. I don't believe what I'm hearing.

"*Second* lowest bidder," Susan says irritably, starting to lose it at last. "And don't tell me you don't do that down here. Earth's entire colonization effort on Mars was contracted to vendors who supplied goods and services at the lowest cost."

I roll my eyes.

Susan ignores it.

"Ben, this is a pointless discussion," she says angrily. "Forget the missiles on the *Kennedy*. There's no reason why they'll ever be deployed. Earth has plenty of room for Americans from Mars."

"There's no such thing as Americans from Mars."

Susan scowls deeply and stares at me. I put on an ornery face to match my ornery words.

"Are you really that parochial, Ben?" Susan replies. "*No one* ever said we weren't Americans just because we went to Mars." No one on Mars anyway, I think, and keep my ornery face on. "For Pete's sake," Susan cries. "Would it make you feel better if we called ourselves Martian-Americans? Or Martians of American descent?"

"How about if we talk about this again when your goddamn Martian missiles aren't pointing at us?" I holler back.

That slows down Susan. But it doesn't quite stop her.

TALL WAR

"They're not *my* missiles, Ben," she says, her tone noticeably milder. "They are strictly just-in-case weapons. You know, the kinds of things you use when the other guy would rather blow your space capsule up then talk about why you're here?" That heats Susan right back up again. She starts yelling. "Have you been listening to anything I've been saying, Ben?"

I sure have. How *else* did I get so wound up? Both of us are having simultaneous fits, though that's not going to get anything resolved. It's my turn to thumb down the knob toward reasonable.

"Susan, I *have* been listening," I tell her earnestly. "I'm sorry if you don't think I have. Maybe I just don't get everything."

Susan's face softens.

"Forgive me, Ben. My getting frustrated isn't going to help anything. It's just that with Gary and Malcolm both dead this whole mission got shoved on my plate."

"And I'm sorry for that," I say and mean it. Gary might have lost his partner, but Susan lost her lover and *both* of her teammates. That causes an old itch in my brain that hasn't been scratched. "You said earlier that Saint Jean was Gary's partner," I say. "Yet you were sleeping with him. Malcolm had to know about that, right?"

"Yes. Gary and Malcolm were partners—business, sports, best of friends—they shared everything except sex and babies."

"They weren't homosexuals?"

"No way. Anyone can have sex. But only partners are responsible for each other."

"Do some men have female partners?"

"Some. But because there are a lot fewer women than men on Mars, other males are allowed to have sex with them."

"Bummer."

Susan grins, but she doesn't comment.

"So, you were sleeping with Gary and he asked you to drop whatever you were doing and come with him to Earth?"

"Close. I am a trained spacer *and* Gary asked me to come along."

"And you did. Just like that. I find that kind of amazing."

"Yes? Well, that's how it was."

Before I can wrap my head around Susan's tales of who sleeps with who on Mars and why, something seizes me and rips me right off her lap. Some animal has grabbed me in its jaws. Its breath is sour and hot. It tightens its grip enough to squeeze the air out of my lungs. Then it digs its rear claws into Susan's leg and jumps.

Whatever has a hold of me isn't going anywhere, however. Talbot has it by the tail. The animal struggles wildly, then it drops me, rears back, and sinks its teeth into Susan's hand. I fall hard to the ground. Talbot curses and releases its tail.

The hunter stops and eyes me. It is a large red fox with mange. It has lost a lot of hair around its neck and shoulders. Or is that a sign that it is infected with a more dangerous disease? Not that I will necessarily live to be affected by whatever it is if the fox manages to drag me away. The animal leaps for me. Bam! Once again, I am in its jaws.

It spins around looking for the direction to its den. That turns out to be a mistake. If the fox had bolted straight away after grabbing me, I would have been a goner. But because it took time to orient itself toward the direction of its underground home, Talbot gets the fraction of a second she needs to dive at the fox again. She seizes its tail with both hands.

TALL WAR

The fox refuses to drop me this time, scratching wildly at Susan with its front claws. Talbot takes some deep scratches, but manages to get back up on her knees. She swings the fox by its own tail and bashes its head onto the ground. Amazingly, the animal still struggles to escape with me still in its mouth. The iron-headed little bastard. Susan puts her foot on its neck and steps down hard. I can hear bones break and a soft sigh as the dying fox releases its last breath. Its jaws go slack and I crawl away.

Talbot is looking at the dead fox, but not seeing me.

"Susan?" I call out.

"Where are you?" she asks. "Can you come closer to the fire?" It is dark now, but the fire is only a few steps away.

I walk over. Susan sees me, picks me up gently, and sits back down by the fire. She sets me on her thigh.

"Are you all right?" she asks.

"I am."

I am soaked with fox spit—an odor akin to wet dog hair—but that will wash off. All things considered, I got off lightly.

"How bad is your hand?" I ask Talbot.

Susan looks at where the fox has scratched and bit her. I look, too. The little fighter gnawed her palm pretty well. "It doesn't look like anything is severed," Susan says. "The bleeding is slowing. What the hell was that bastard's problem? Stubborn little prick."

"I can't say. It's a red fox and that animal has a reputation for being smart."

Talbot just shakes her head.

"Thanks for reacting so quickly," I tell her. "You saved my life."

Susan nods. Then she takes some things out of one of the pouches on her belt. She gives herself an inoculation directly into her palm using a pen injector. She opens and applies some sort of antiseptic ointment to her wound, then she wraps gauze around her hand and tapes it up.

Talbot looks at me.

"And how about you?" she asks. "You took a big fall. Anything get hurt?"

"My left shoulder hurts."

"Lift your arm," Susan tells me. I do. I yelp in discomfort. "Try rotating it," she says.

Ow, shit. I can't.

"I think my shoulder is dislocated," I tell her.

"Unzip and pull down your sleeve so I can see."

"I can't do it."

"Stand still," she says. Talbot unzips my RediMedi to the waist and pulls my left arm out of the sleeve. That is so painful I want to scream. But I don't. I have some pride. Susan presses her finger against my left shoulder. I scream as loud as I can.

"You're right. The ball has been jerked out of the socket." Talbot looks at me. "I'm trained to fix things like this. Would you like me to try?"

"If I say please don't, will you leave it alone?" I whine.

"No. I just won't ask you a second time."

"Are you sure you can fix it?" I ask, not happy about what's coming.

"Sit down and shut up."

Susan lifts my arm with one hand and presses against my shoulder with the other. Then she yanks my arm straight down. I shriek like a banshee. Then I pass out. When I wake up, I am inside Talbot's chest pocket. Arms and legs tucked down at the bottom seam. Chest and face resting against her breast. She is walking through the forest at first light. My penis is hard as a rock.

"Hello," Susan says seeing that I'm awake. "How's the shoulder?"

I rotate it gingerly.

"Feels like you got it put back right," I admit. "How's your hand?"

"Painfully sore. Or I'd give you a hand job."

It's obvious what she's teasing me about, but I refuse to acknowledge it. She laughs and walks on. Her breast bounces as she hikes, and her nipple pokes at me beneath her suit. And I thought I was hard before.

CHAPTER 24

Susan finds more wild blackberries for breakfast. She says that an adult brown bear was picking the same patch but ignored her. He's lucky she didn't neutron him. Bear steaks. Bear roast. Barbeque bear. Bear jerky.

We eat the blackberries and talk about the fact that we have to cross the Potomac to get to my farm on the Virginia side. Susan is sure she can make it across the river, which I find somewhat incredible since she doesn't know how to swim. She tells me that she loves water and did just fine when she landed in the Potomac. Fine, I tell her. Fine. Do what you want. As for me, I'll be hiking to the first Maryland village I come to and hopping on an ElecT. We make plans to rendezvous in the wooded area south of Alexandria seaport the next morning.

Surprisingly, everything works out. We meet up a little after noon the following day. Susan wasn't too hard to spot. She was the giant carrying two salmon. We pick a sheltered place in the forest to spend the last daylight hours. And Susan tosses up

TALL WAR

another of her cooking racks. She cleans the fish in the Potomac and returns with several large pink filets. The salmon cooks over the fire while Talbot and I talk about what we're going to do when we get to Washington.

She wants to clarify her status. Is she a visitor? Or an unwanted alien? Will she be allowed to stay, accommodating her Original-size body to our Final-size world? Or will she be quarantined somewhere? I nod. I listen. But I'm actually thinking about Talbot's mother ship orbiting above us. The MSS John F. Kennedy armed to the teeth with things known to be harmful to human health and well-being.

While Susan drones on and on about what she hopes to experience in our world, I try to figure how I can get to Geness's dad, Carmel Wilson. My hope is that Mr. Wizard can hack into the *Kennedy's* programming and freeze its missiles. Tizzle, twazzle, twozzle, twome!

I obviously don't share what I'm thinking with Talbot. Sure, I feel bad that her companions were killed. And yes, I feel disloyal hoping Carmel will be able to chop into her spaceship's computer when she has been so wonderful to me. But I'm worried about the missiles on her ship and the fact that they can be controlled by personnel back on Mars. Maybe Wilson could simply turn the spaceship around and aim the missiles back at the Lewis and Clark Colony. Of course, that's a ridiculous thought. And he very likely could never get it to fly all the way back to Mars. But that doesn't stop me from liking the idea.

Susan and I stay hidden in the woods, resting until dark. Then we set out for my dairy. I am happy to be going home, yet the closer I get the more stressed I become, imagining that another group of Rigging Nash's agents will be waiting there.

Granted, I'm not wearing working netacts and therefore I'm not broadcasting a come-shoot-me signal to whomever Nash might have dispatched to replace the late Adrian Modigliarty. But we will pass close to other farms, and there is a danger that Susan will be seen and reported before I can get ahold of Geness or her father.

Talbot hikes steadily through the night with me tucked into her breast pocket again. And long before my erection subsides *or morning dawns*, we arrive at the edge of the woods that borders my farm. How lonely the familiar shapes of its buildings seem by the light of the crescent moon. I hate that the house is dark. Gen always kept a light on outside, telling the world that our little farmhouse was safe and welcoming. There is no light tonight. That makes me instantly sad. And angry, too. How much longer will I be separated from my wife and son?

"Let me make sure that no one's home," I tell Susan. "Then we'll head to the barn."

"Roger that," Talbot replies and sets me down. "I need to duck into the woods for a little while anyway."

"Blackberries?" I ask her.

"What?"

"Never mind."

I cut across the yard toward the house and open the front door. It's never locked. I go in. Everything is quiet inside. I leave the lights off and walk into the kitchen. I open the fridge. No fresh items. No baby food for Lodge. Nothing's been added or removed for days. I go upstairs. Everything is tidy and neat. I look in Gen's closet. A lot of her work clothes have been taken. Mostly presidential things. She's probably working at the Oval Office around the clock, juggling whatever crises have brewed

TALL WAR

up since the space capsule's destruction and the death of its crew. Plus trying to locate me, or my body.

I strip off my suit and take a shower. I pull a new, blue RediMedi out of my closet. I put it on and activate its systems by allowing it to take a sample of my blood. I get fresh socks and yank my faithful cowboy boots back on. Even in the dark they look a little worse for wear. But wear is what they were made for, and as much crap as they've taken the last few days, they haven't let me down. One more reason I love cows. I grab a new box of netacts out of the bathroom medicine cabinet and head downstairs. Man, I'd love to take just five more minutes and make some coffee, but it's already getting light out.

I glance at my watch. It's almost six o'clock in the morning. Someone should be over here milking the cows. Gen wouldn't forget about that. I go out the back door of the house and head for the barn. I look for Talbot, but I don't see her. Probably wasn't the blackberries. She's likely clogged up her plumbing eating all that meat. Next thing you know I'll be searching for Magicmucil in bulk.

I head toward the barn, big and red in the early morning light. It's as impressive today as it was when an old-time Original built it new for *his* dairy cows. I reach for the handle of the small door I installed next to the Original's door when I am suddenly hurled against the barn by a massive explosion behind me. I look back and stare at a fireball where my home used to be. Some shithead has blown up my house! My adrenaline hits big time and I am furious. Who the hell is trying to kill me now?

Susan comes running out of the woods as flaming pieces of my house drop everywhere. She's clutching a pair of Finals in her right hand. She tosses them to the ground. Two boney, mean-as-shit security agents are tied together with some kind of black cord that Talbot has spun around them like a spider's thread. *New* fems with the same bad attitude as the *old* ones.

"These bitches took out your home, Ben," Susan says enraged. "I'm sorry I didn't see them skulking in the trees until after the deed was done." She looks at the raging fire, which is burning up the remnants of my house. "Is anyone going to respond to that?" Talbot asks.

"No. Farmers are on their own. However, there should have been someone here milking the cows."

Talbot nods. Then she bends down and grabs both of the women. She lifts them up and holds them inches from her face.

"It's time to tell your story, people," Susan says. She's trying to speak normally but the cold fury in her voice is stark. I think it's the scariest sound I have ever heard.

CHAPTER 25

Talbot pinches one of the females' heads between her thumb and forefinger.

"Tell me," she says squeezing. The woman screams in agony. "Tell me!" Talbot demands and squeezes harder. I decide not to watch. I don't get even twenty feet away when I see a body lying in the grass. I recognize who it is. Gen had indeed asked someone she trusted to take care of my cows. Turns out it was poor Stratsen Yun, a young, hired hand from Olnee Anderson's nearby farm.

Yun lies sprawled on his back. His eyes are open and curious. Probably wondering what the women approaching him want. The small black laser hole in his forehead is the answer he never saw coming. It shot a hole out of the back of his head and a lot of his blood has leaked out. I stare at the gentle soul who has been reduced to zero. And he wasn't even the real target. Just a farmhand in the wrong place at the wrong time. There's a lot of that going around right now. I'm so sorry, Stratsen. I'll take care of my cows, then I'll return and take care of you.

I go back and tell Susan that the agents killed one of my neighbors. Both fems are lying on the ground now. They're watching silently. Talbot holds out her palm and shows me a pair of laser pistols she took away from them.

"Be careful," I tell her. "Those killers may well be wearing suits capable of injecting poison. Or of blowing up themselves *and* you."

Susan nods.

"I'll watch out," she says grimly. "But let me assure you that these two bad-ass girls are going to tell me what I want to know."

Farewell ladies, is all I can think as I head for the barn again. I go inside and turn on the floodlights. I call out to my girls and get affectionate greetings in return. They are skittish from the explosions and wary with fire so near. I chat with each one of them, reassuring them while I perform our shared rituals of feeding and milking.

In the end, none of the cows appear the worse for wear. Still, I'll add extra oats to their feedboxes this morning, and toss in a few dried apples as well. I am overwhelmed by how happy I am just getting to do my everyday chores again. Gosh, wouldn't it be great if I could somehow forget all the space stuff and just stay here? Of course, that's out of the question now. Maybe forever.

I finish up and walk back to Susan. She is kneeling on the ground. She hears me coming and calls out, "Go away."

I stop.

"You okay?" I ask her.

"I'm fine. Come back in five minutes."

What the hey? If she's still working on the two security fems there's nothing she can do to them that would earn my disapproval. I ignore Susan's warning and walk up. Both agents are lying motionless on the ground. Naked. Their suits have been stripped off and tossed to the side. It appears that their arms and legs have been broken. And their eyes poked out. I should be throwing up, but I'm not.

"What happened?" I ask.

"Tough couple of broads," Talbot tells me.

"Not that tough," I comment. "You were able to kill them."

"It took a lot of encouragement to get them to tell me what we needed to know. But they did." Talbot looks at me. "Does the name Dung Tro set off any alarms?"

Once upon a time Geness had to remind me who he was. Not now.

"He's the current president of the United Nations Security Council," I respond.

Talbot grimaces and shakes her head, more distressed by that news than by the broken bodies of the two agents she tortured and killed to get it.

"He's the power behind Rigging Nash and his cunt rangers," Talbot goes on, furious. "Acting on his own authority, Tro personally gave the order for the capsule to be destroyed and the crew murdered. His actions were denounced today as a breach of his powers by both the Security Council and the General Assembly. By majority votes in each body he was stripped of his office."

"Majority?" I yelp. "Why not unanimous?"

Talbot asked the agents that question.

"The Three Chinas all voted to retain Tro, claiming that his actions were authorized by emergency powers granted to the Council president."

"Including permission to murder visitors from outer space?" I ask rhetorically.

"Never know when you'll get a snootful of alien," is Susan's take. "Do you want to know how the authorities found out about Tro's culpability?"

"His what?" I ask.

"His guilt," Talbot translates. "You will be familiar with the characters involved." Susan winks, then she continues. "Complete logs of Tro's orders—encryptions decoded and texts translated—were distributed to the members of the Security Council and the ambassadors to the UN by the president of the United States."

Susan smiles.

"Geness is fine, by the way, and is being protected by troops reporting to General Wainwright. Though he sustained multiple injuries falling to the ground after the first capsule blast, I am happy to report that he is recovering and retains command of the United Nations forces deployed under him at the capsule landing site.

"Geness not only provided transcripts documenting Dung Tro's betrayal, but she has formed a coalition of nations in the UN that is demanding that he be arrested and tried for his actions." Talbot pauses. "I'm glad your wife is all right, Ben. You should know that she's had search parties looking everywhere for you ever since the attack on the *Jon Jon*. And guess what else?" Susan grins with almost goofy delight. "Gary survived!"

I laugh out loud I am so surprised and delighted. The intrepid captain of the *Kennedy* is still alive! He is one lucky son of a bitch. The news of his survival is the high point of an afternoon full of astounding news. Dung Tro's murderous behaviors have been outed. Rigging Nash has been proved a traitor. And Admiral Gary Friedman has defied fate and dodged the attempt to wipe out the spacemen from Mars.

Susan has more.

"Apparently in an effort to support the UN coalition demanding Dung Tro's detainment, Gary today revealed the existence of the mother ship."

"Did he tell about the missiles, too?"

"Yes, he did—claiming accurately I might add—that he has in his possession a command chip that allows him to remotely access the *Kennedy's* computers and direct armed missiles to any target he chooses. He warned Dung Tro that he would use them to support Geness and the United Nations, after she had made it very clear to Tro that his only option was to surrender himself to UN authorities."

"Awesome," I murmur. That's *my* Gen she's talking about. Turns out that bed is not the only place where the lady is a tiger.

CHAPTER 26

"We have to get out of here," I tell Talbot. "Dung Tro has known about us from the moment you intercepted his agents."

"Do you really think he's still going to pursue you after all of this?"

Do bears shit blackberries in the woods?

"Tro is ambassador from Beijing and allied to all Three Chinas," I explain. "Those nations account for half the population of the planet and three-quarters of its economy. Just because his covert activities have been identified and his powers threatened, it doesn't mean for a minute that he's going to step down peacefully. He may well attempt to pull a coup at the United Nations and take on *all* of the world government's powers.

"Gen is leading the opposition against him, which also makes me a continuing target. While I'm not foolish enough to think that Dung gives a flying fuck about Ben the dairyman, I'm guessing he would like to capture or kill Ben, the president's *husband*. He's already sent two sets of agents after me. Why should he stop now?

TALL WAR

"Having said all that, I don't think I am really the one Dung is after. I'm sure the two agents you just sent to hell got off vids of you to their handler, and thus to Tro, proving that *you* are still alive. You and Gary are the most important targets anywhere on the planet. If he can dispose of you two, there will be no spacers from Mars to deal with."

"So where do we go?" Susan asks anxiously. "The White House?"

"I really wish we could," I say. "But we'd never make it that far now that Dung Tro knows exactly where we are. I think we should try to get to Gen's parents, who live close to here. I must warn you that it might also occur to Tro that's where we might go. But he won't be able to get there before we do and we'll find some way to protect ourselves.

"Gen's dad is the genius who's been intercepting and breaking Tro's encryptions. He and Gen's mother live in an Original-size house preserved from the days when America was a brand-new nation. Almost a thousand years ago now. Washington slept there. Jefferson slept there. No reason why you and I shouldn't sleep there."

"Let's do it," Susan says, probably wondering who the hell Washington and Jefferson were.

"Another plus," I add, "is that Wilson, Gen's father, has all of his technology installed at the house so he can put us directly in touch with Gen and Gary and let them know we're alive."

Talbot shakes her head slowly and holds her hand up as if to stop me.

"No word to Gary," she says in a pensive tone. "Not quite yet anyway. Right now, he doesn't think there's anyone looking over his shoulder. Good place for me to keep an eye on him."

"But he's helping Geness," I remind her.

"He is for *now*, Ben," she says. "But in the long run, Gary is obliged to follow his mission charter. He has to make sure that the people of Mars can return to this world. It's why he came here. He'll support Gen for now, but only as long as it is in his best interest to get his greater goal accomplished." Talbot pauses for a moment, then resumes speaking slowly, picking and choosing her words carefully. "Gary is not a diplomat, Ben. He was picked for the Martian return to Earth because he's a conquistador." Susan gazes at me. "Do you remember them?"

Do I? I loved those guys when I was a kid. Blunderbusses. Cool pointy hats. Nerves of steel. I devoured the stories of Pizarro and Cortes, Coronado and Orellana, until I got old enough to read the fine print about their heroics. Pillage and murder. Rape and looting. Disease and starvation. Broke my heart. And now Talbot has flat out acknowledged that Gary is a conquistador. It's not a compliment.

"I remember who they were," is all I tell her.

"Then you know *exactly* what Gary can and will do," Susan says bluntly.

"He didn't come across like that when I was with him," I protest.

"Trust me on this," Susan says firmly.

I stare at her for a moment, confused that such a charming man could harbor such terrible demons.

"And you slept with that guy?" I ask.

Susan nods.

"Even Pizarro had a wife," she tells me.

There's that. Though it doesn't seem like much of a justification for Susan to have spent fifty million miles putting out for Gary.

TALL WAR

"We need to get out of here, Susan," I tell her again. "My in-laws live only a couple of miles from here."

"Look," Talbot responds. "Why don't you head there on your own and stay low. I'll wait back here in the woods. If all hell doesn't break loose at your in-laws, we can connect when you return to milk your cows tonight."

"You know about cows?" I ask surprised.

"No," Talbot answers. "But I listened when you talked about them. I know how important your animals are to you." Susan gives me a rare tender smile. "Just like animals are important to me." Her smile turns to a guilty grin. "Is there anything to hunt in these woods?"

I can't help but laugh.

"There are deer," I tell her.

"Whitetail?"

"You know about deer, too?"

"I know about meat."

"How are you going to cook it without alerting the universe?"

"I can contain the smoke."

"You're sure?"

Talbot gives me a thumbs up.

"That means up your ass around here," I tell her. "Did you know that?"

Susan just grins.

"By the way, if I'm late getting back here, you can hang out in the barn. Cows might be a little cranky, though, so remember to stand clear."

"I understand. I'm like that when I don't get laid."

"Too much information. Also, just in case you're interested, all the cows are girls."

"Don't be disgusting."

"See you tonight."

Susan gives me a thumbs up again.

Ha.

I think of one more thing.

"Gary said that he has a chip in his possession that can remotely access the *Kennedy's* missiles. Is that true?"

"Yes. It's implanted inside of his body. He can retrieve it to link up to the ship's computer systems."

Implanted? Like the ID chips folks used to stick in their pets? I wonder *what* the Mars men planted inside Gary's body. At the very least they would have had to make sure that he would be able to dig it out by himself if he had to use it. Given what Susan has told me about Gary, the rest of the Martians—fifty million miles away and in the dark as to the status of their crew's mission—may well have put it just out of Gary's reach to prevent him from acting on his own. If the mission authorities have used even a modicum of caution, Friedman would have to have help from another astronaut, *and* likely their consent for any planned confrontation with Earth authorities.

"Was Gary the only member of the crew implanted with a chip?" I ask.

"No," Susan replies. "Malcolm was implanted with a back-up chip. But only Gary knew where it was embedded in Saint Jean's body."

I frown. This whole thing is getting…well, icky.

"So, the *Kennedy's* first officer carried a back-up chip—the key to the nukes as it were—but its implanted location *in his body* was kept from him because no one in the corridors of powers trusted him to know when to retrieve it?"

TALL WAR

Talbot makes a disapproving face.

"It's not as mindlessly bureaucratic as all that," she snaps at me. Talbot's defensive salvo reveals, of course, that it's exactly that. "If something happened to Gary, or to his chip," Susan goes on, "then Mal would have been told by Mission Control how to locate and extract the back-up chip."

"Mission Control," I murmur. That is the name of my favorite space vid series on television. Mission Control is NASA-speak for the all-knowing, all-powerful executive management of the space agency. Which leads me directly to the most important question of this conversation. I watch Susan's face carefully, and then I ask it. "Do you think Gary will contact Mars before he retrieves and activates the chip?"

"Ha! Do conquistadors ask for permission?" she rebuts, contempt for Gary's recklessness etched onto her features. But then she answers me seriously, seeing my genuine concern. "No. He won't ask."

"Well, thank God for that. Keeps Mission Control off our backs."

"Yes," Susan says. "Not that God cares."

Susan gives me a questioning glance. Is she waiting for me to respond? To jump in and
take my own swipe at a distant deity. I don't. I personally am not confident enough to write God off. But I have to admit that I love atheists. You can count on them to do what they have to do. They know there is no one else out there to bail them out. They not only expect to have to take care of things, but *they expect to do it by themselves*. Unless they are lucky enough to have the help of a loving spouse. Or a brave friend. Or a dairy farmer in over his head.

CHAPTER 27

"Fuck me!" Corkabee exclaims when she sees me standing outside her door. I can't tell if she's relieved or disappointed until she hugs me and starts crying. "You're alive," she sobs, and holds me close. She's wearing navy shorts and a white blouse. Her feet are bare.

"Thank you, Corky," I say and pull away gently. I look at her face. Her eyes are bloodshot. Has she been crying, fearing me dead? Oh, God, I suddenly panic. Has something happened to Geness?

"Is Gen all right?" I ask. Corkabee nods, wiping her eyes with the back of her hand. "I need to talk to Wilson right away," I tell her. "It's critical!"

Cory's eyes go big, but she doesn't challenge my request. She leaves me on the front porch and literally runs to tell him I'm here. I step inside and activate a mechanical draw that pulls the Original-size door shut.

Wilson appears in moments and stops dead at the sight of me. He is wearing a white lab coat. Not your usual geek wear.

TALL WAR

Maybe he's doing some antistatic work. Or he just likes how he looks in it. He stares at me.

"Where have you been?" he asks, completely dumbfounded that I have turned up on his doorstep.

"I'll tell you everything," I say. "But please, I have to contact Gen and tell her I'm alive."

"Of course, dear boy," Wilson says looking at me. "You need nourishment and a bath."

"What I need is to call Gen," I insist.

"We'll do that, I promise," Wilson assures me. "But if you don't want Gen to fret when she sees you a clean-up is required. It will only take a few minutes."

Corkabee leads me to the bathroom in her master bedroom and gets me set with soap and a borrowed razorblade from Wilson. I shave, shower, pull on my RediMedi, and head back to the kitchen. It is a Final-size kitchen with appliances and a mahogany table and chairs. It has been built into one corner of the massive colonial kitchen, a cavernous brick-and-mortar affair filled with chains and hooks, and iron pots. It looks like a medieval torture chamber. Back in the day it probably functioned exactly that way for the unfortunate animals brought here.

"I called Gen from a secure line in my study," Wilson tells me immediately. "She answered in the middle of a conference with UN Security Council members. She said she would call back in a half hour or so." My father-in-law pauses and looks at me with a serious expression. "I did not tell her about you. That's your privilege."

I nod gratefully. I've missed my wife terribly and ached for her not knowing that I survived the destruction of the spaceship.

The absence of my dead body was the lone, dark seed of hope that maybe I had not died in the capsule blasts.

Corkabee tells Wilson and me to sit. She serves coffee and gets to work on a light supper for us. At Wilson's urging I tell him my story. Starting all the way back at the conversation I had with Geness about rounding up fresh food for the Martian spacemen sitting in their vessel floating in the Potomac. I tell Wilson about meeting General Wainwright. And how I got myself invited into the space capsule to talk with its commander, Gary Friedman.

Corky serves us ham sandwiches and homemade potato salad. I eat and drink cup after cup of coffee, talking the whole time. I'm sure I've spooned enough sugar into my coffees to make my RediMedi check its insulin reserves.

I give Wilson and Corkabee all the details I can think of, not having realized how desperate I am to have someone hear what happened to me. I describe how I saw Rigging Nash's spies aboard the space capsule. How it got blown up and I got tossed into the Potomac. Corky gets up and makes another stack of sandwiches. I talk on and on.

I tell them about the turtle that grabbed me in Chesapeake Bay and how I was miraculously rescued by the astronaut, Susan Talbot. And how she promptly saved me again when Nash's boogeyman, Adrian Modigliarty, tracked me down using my netacts' signal. When I tell Wilson and Corky about Talbot stepping on Modigliarty, Corkabee drops her knife on the floor.

Wilson and I look at her. She's as pale as a blanched almond. She picks up the knife, washes it off, and pretends like nothing happened. Then she promptly drops it again when I share what Talbot did to extract information from the two security fems who

TALL WAR

blew up my house. At last, I am wound down, having shared everything from A to Z in the saga of the dairyman in distress.

"Ben," Wilson says when I finish. "I am glad that you made it through all your adventures."

"*Adventures?*" Corkabee responds, her voice topping off in a high-pitched sarcastic squeak. She sets a new tray of sandwiches on the table. "Ben survived one disaster after another. Give credit when credit is due, Wilson. He's been through things that you and I can't even imagine."

I smile in embarrassment. Wilson just nods. Corky smiles at me. Then she hugs me again.

"I admire your courage," Wilson says, making an effort to put a little meat on the bone. "And I sincerely applaud your enviable record of survival. I really don't think I'm acquainted with another person who could have overcome all those obstacles. Well done, son."

I feel embarrassed again, but Wilson spares me any more compliments. Corky smiles, happy now. Wilson gets back to business.

"We have to prepare for Gen's call. You'll need to activate the replacement netacts you grabbed when you were at the farm. However," Wilson's eyes narrow and his voice turns very serious, "because they're registered to you, the first thing your netacts will do is to inform the Cloud of your GPS location. Now we don't want that, do we?" Wilson shakes his head. "Please hand them to me. I'll jailbreak them and fix that issue."

I unzip a pocket on my RediMedi and hand Wilson a small, plastic slab with a new set of netacts lenses vacuum-sealed inside.

"What exactly are you going to do?" I ask.

"I'm going to safeguard your ID."

I thought only gangsters and telemarketers knew how to do that.

"Where did you learn that?"

"Actually, I developed the procedure to do it," Wilson answers with a wee bit of pride in his voice. "The military wanted to prevent enemy soldiers from readily identifying officers or specific combatants intercepting their netacts transmissions. So, I designed a transistor gate that disassembles—if you will—the ID signal as it passes through, erasing its data.

"Today those kind of netacts are worn by every soldier in the UN. To be sure, the gate can also be neutralized, ending its sanitizing activity in case of injury or death so that the owner can be located." Corkabee shivers when she hears that. Wilson notices. "It's an important feature," he declares. Cork just shakes her head.

"I'll be back in just a few minutes," he says, rising from his chair. He pauses for just a moment and looks at me. "She wouldn't let anyone talk about you like you were dead, you know," Gen's father tells me, his voice husky with emotion. "'He's missing,' she would say. 'He's missing.'"

I nod, grateful for those words, and suddenly I feel so emotional that I have to work hard not to let the tears out that I've pushed back every time I thought Gen might have given up on ever seeing me again. And, hugs notwithstanding, I am not yet ready to cry in front of my mother-in-law. Wilson turns away and heads off to his lab.

Corky pours both of us more coffee, and fills me in on everything Lodge did at her house before Geness took him to the White House to be with her. I love hearing the details, even though they're mostly about accidents, tantrums, messes, and

TALL WAR

poopy pants. I would love to listen to Corkabee explain to Lodge that once upon a time his old dad experienced exactly the same problems.

Wilson comes back. He hands me the netacts slab. "You can put them in," he says. "While you're doing that, I'll take Gen's call and forward it to you."

"Thank you," I tell him. Wilson disappears again. Corky starts washing the dishes and I finish my coffee. I get up from the table and take my empty cup over to her. I stop dead in my tracks. I hear the unmistakable sound of helicopters. I race to the front door with Corkabee on my heels and push the button that opens the full-size Original door. There are at least a dozen black choppers in the distance.

"Corky, get Wilson!" I yell. She stares at me, not comprehending my urgency. "Dung Tro sent those helicopters. He knows I'm here. We have to go now or we're all dead!"

Wilson appears on his own, his face anxious and his forehead perspiring.

"What will they do?" he asks.

"The worst they can," I holler. Then I grab Corky's hand, race through the colonial mansion, and out the backdoor, which has been left open to bring fresh air into the house. Wilson is right behind us and the three of us sprint across the backyard toward the woods that border the grounds. We hide in the trees and watch the helicopters make their final approach. I can see UN flags painted on their snouts.

Suddenly half of the attack group cuts away and heads east toward the District of Columbia. Someone has obviously just decided to target Geness as well. *Kill the president? Impossible!* But it's not impossible. I'm seeing it with my own eyes. The remaining choppers are almost in our face. I turn to run deeper into the woods, but Wilson grabs my arm.

"Wait!" he cries and points to the sky. Above the helicopters roars a four-pack of fighter jets. Moving at fantastic speeds they split up and head down, firing rockets at the UN helicopters. The choppers explode in huge novas of yellow and black smoke. Utterly destroyed before they could get off even a single shot.

Instantly it is raining metal fragments and flaming body parts. I dodge a huge hunk of copter only to be knocked down by what is obviously a severed foot. Then the woods catch on fire as the burning fragments ignite the trees. I yell to Wilson and Corky that we have to get out of the forest or the fire will consume us.

We run like hell for the mansion. It appears undamaged, but fallen flaming debris is everywhere between us and the house, and the air is thick with smoke and ash. We have almost reached the house when we hear a series of terrific explosions from the direction of Washington, DC. Have the other helicopters been intercepted and destroyed? Or have they managed to blow up Gen and the White House? Dear God, what is happening?

CHAPTER 28

Wilson knows. He is standing with Corkabee and me on the back porch staring at the mansion grounds. They are littered with the blazing shells of crashed helicopters and sizzling, stinking piles of flesh from blown-apart corpses. It is a landscape from hell. We stare at the destruction both as horrified observers and grateful survivors. The smell of burning oil and the smoke from the roasting flesh makes us cover our noses and mouths with our hands. Wilson turns to me and talks loudly over the roar of the burning wasteland.

"Gen called and warned me that Dung Tro had dispatched attack copters to our home. She was informed by General Wainwright who told her that he had ordered jets to intercept them."

"What about Gen?" I shout back fearful. "The rest of the helicopters headed for Washington."

"I suspect she is all right," Wilson hollers, "or I would have heard something."

Suddenly a huge explosion blows heat and fire toward us. We take shelter inside the house hoping the old colonial mansion won't be set on fire by the inferno out back.

"I need to rest for a moment," Wilson says and sits in a chair at the table. Corkabee and I sit, too. It's been one hell of a half hour.

"Dung Tro still has significant support in the Security Council and in the General Assembly," Wilson says speaking up. "Many nations are afraid that the Originals' reappearance on Earth is a harbinger of a full-scale invasion to come. And just in time to make things worse, Admiral Friedman went public this morning with the fact that there is a Martian spaceship in Earth orbit armed with twenty-four neutron-tipped missiles."

Wilson shakes his head, disapprovingly.

"*That* created near hysteria in both UN bodies. Ben, are you able to remember what Susan Talbot told you about how Friedman can access those weapons?"

It looks to me that Wilson's need to sit down has to do more with talking to me about Gary's missiles than needing some rest.

"What about my call to Gen?" I ask.

"This will only take a few moments," Wilson promises. "I wouldn't ask if it wasn't critically important."

It seems that every minute something new is critically important. Everything except
me getting to talk to my wife. Wilson stares at me, as intense as I have ever seen him. He repeats his question from a minute ago.

"Please tell me what you can remember concerning Admiral Friedman's ability to remotely access the computers on the mother ship using a communications device in his possession. Every detail is important, Ben. *Every detail.*"

"Talbot told me that Friedman has a command chip embedded in his body. When he retrieves it, he will be able to log into and directly access the *Kennedy's* systems."

"And he's the only one with a chip?"

"Malcolm Saint Jean—the spaceman who was killed in the capsule explosions—had one, too. It was the designated back-up to Friedman's."

"So, Talbot doesn't have one?"

"She said the only ones were implanted in Friedman and Saint Jean."

Wilson frowns and thinks about that.

"My guess is that she actually has one, too," he finally states. "Mission Control on Mars would make sure that Friedman had access to *multiple* back-up chips seeing how important the chip would be to the astronauts once they had left the mother ship."

I understand.

"Like I said, Susan only told me about chips being embedded in Friedman and Saint Jean."

"Then I suspect she is lying. Or perhaps, she was implanted without her knowledge," Wilson suggests.

I don't think Susan would lie. But what do I know? If she *is* withholding the truth, then why did she ever tell me about the chip at all? As to whether she carries a chip implanted in her body without her knowledge, *that* has a ring of truth considering the furtive politics behind the Martian return to Earth. If you don't have any qualms sending twenty-four neutron bombs to be used on an unsuspecting world, you sure as hell won't mind planting one chip in an unsuspecting spacer.

"Ben, I have to get my hands on one of those chips," Wilson

tells me sounding urgent. "And whether Talbot knows she has one embedded or not, she is my only prospect."

"I'll ask her."

"You'll *ask* her?" Wilson repeats, as though my remark is somehow inane.

"Yeah. I'm not going to call her a liar," I protest. "I'll explain that you believe a chip may have been implanted in her body without her knowledge and I'll see what she says."

"That's your plan?" Wilson asks, not trying to hide his skepticism.

"Pretty much."

Wilson frowns but leaves me alone. I don't think Susan knows she has a chip. When I tell her about Wilson's suspicion I don't think the news will jar her very much. She learned way back on her own world that there were rules for Gary, and there were other rules for her.

Wilson is fidgeting, tapping the desk with his fingers.

"What?" I ask him.

"Tell Talbot that I can detect the implant if she is willing to let me look for it."

"I don't know why she would give us the chip," I counter. "Wouldn't that make her a traitor?"

"What?" Wilson responds. "Her finding out whether or not she is carrying a chip would do no such thing."

"You're right," I tell Wilson. "I was skipping ahead to the part where we tell her that you want to take it out. *That's* the part she's going to have a problem with. Although even just learning that it exists might give her a little leverage in dealing with Friedman. Especially in light of the fact that she suspects her commander might have secret orders to judge the Earth's capability to defend itself against a Martian invasion."

TALL WAR

Wilson is shocked. His face looks like the electric utility has just cut off power to his lab.

"What?" he sputters, barely able to speak.

"Apparently the admiral's we-come-in-peace gesture was real enough," I answer. "But Talbot suspects that the Martian authorities have privately authorized Gary *to pursue whatever actions are necessary* to secure the rights for Martians to return to Earth."

"That's a little different than suggesting a Martian invasion," Wilson says, resenting my earlier choice of words.

"I won't quibble," I say. "But bringing along a couple dozen nuclear missiles on their mission to get us to say, sure, you can move in with us, would seem to suggest that the Martians have already made up their minds that they're coming here whether we like it or not. If that's not an invasion, then for sure it's coercion."

"Okay, Ben," Wilson says at last. "Now that I've heard Talbot's concerns about Friedman's secret charter, it simply makes it more urgent than ever that we find out whether she is carrying a chip. It is likely the only real leverage we will have with Friedman."

"Fair enough," I tell him. "I'm going back to the farm to milk my cows this afternoon and meet Talbot at the farm. I promise to put on a full-court press. Before that, however, I am going to call my wife."

Wilson nods.

"Go put in your netacts and I'll go to my study," he says. "Meet me when you're done and we'll make the call." He gets up and leaves. His *study* as he calls it. I've seen it. His work place is an electronics lab at least as large as Thomas Edison's invention central in Menlo Park. Man, would that old boy have loved to have seen all of Wilson's high-tech toys. On the other hand, my father-in-law supports information services for the entire United States, so it's not all play.

I use a mirror in one of the mansion's Final-size restrooms and insert my new pair of netacts. Just thicker than skin—but several magnitudes more durable—they identify the DNA on the surface of my eye and activate themselves. I hurry to meet Wilson who is preparing to initiate a call to Geness on a secure line that I will transfer to my netacts. I am thrilled that this is finally happening, but I won't let myself get too amped up until I see who answers the phone—my wife, or the president of the United States.

CHAPTER 29

I walk into Wilson's lab. It always reminds me of going to a geek's favorite gadget warehouse. There are metal tables with computer monitors spread out in a big circle around the room like the pillars of Stonehenge. There are open cabinets and shelves bolted to the walls full of tools, components, routers, spools of old-fashioned insulated wire, servers in stacks, standalone CPUs, hulking mainframes with air conditioning units blowing chilled air on them, and finally—in the very heart of it all—an old metal desk where Wilson rules this kingdom seated on an antique wooden chair.

Its desktop is covered with an array of additional monitors that bathe Wilson's Holy of Holies in high-definition light. There is no art. No magnets. No day-by-day Garfield calendars. In fact, there isn't anything that doesn't serve a useful *electronic* purpose in Wilson's nirvana. I don't even see the old *Futurama* litho I got him for his fiftieth birthday. It was a rowdy print of the Planet Express crew cavorting on the Nude Beach Planet. In an expensive lapse of judgment, I thought a framed picture of Amy's perky butt, or some Leela side boob, would bring a little erotic irreverence to his sterile nerd haven. But no. I don't see the print anywhere. Not even leaning forgotten against some table leg.

Wilson tells me to pull a chair up to his desk while he opens the secure line to Gen. When she answers, he shoots me the feed and brings her image up on a color monitor in front of me. He shoves his chair to the side and waves me closer. I move my chair right up in front of the screen and sit down. I hold my breath and watch my wife's lovely face appear. She looks anxious and hopeful, and when she sees me she tears up and whispers, "I knew I would see you again."

I can't speak for a moment.

"Us dairy guys don't go down easy," I finally manage to croak.

Geness barely smiles, but I can see that she is truly relieved that I am okay.

"I love you, Benedict," she says softly.

"I love you, Gen."

"I can't imagine what you've been through, my poor boy," she says and wipes away her happy tears.

"I'm still around," I tell her cheerfully. "And that's all that counts. Astronaut Susan Talbot survived as well," I add.

"Yes. Wilson told me how many times she saved your skinny behind." Geness arches an eyebrow. A sure sign of suspicion. "Does she have a crush on you?"

"No," I reply, shaking my head. "She's got the hots for Gary Friedman."

"That's good, because you're taken."

"Speaking of Gary—"

TALL WAR

"He is beside himself that Susan is still alive," Geness interrupts. "He was sure that she'd been killed when the space capsule blew. Not that he would talk much about her disappearance. He's too professional. But when he heard that she had survived he literally let out some kind of war whoop." Gen smiles kindly.

Talbot is not going to be happy to hear this. She didn't want Friedman to know quite yet that she was still around. For my own part, it's hard not to feel happy for Gary. Secret motives—or no secret motives—he was always nice to me. Further, he has continuously supported my wife, even against Dung Tro. The *only* side of him that I've ever seen has been helpful and gracious. On the other hand, I suppose Cortes had Aztec friends right up until he destroyed their whole world.

"How is Lodge?" I ask, changing the subject and the focus of my thoughts. "Can I say hi?"

"He's fine," Geness reassures me. "He misses his daddy. I have him staying with Sheridan and Callie Oakes in Georgetown. Away from any danger."

I am crushed that Lodge is not present. But I don't let Geness see it.

"That was wise," I tell her. "We saw the helicopters targeting you."

"What a stupid move that was," Geness comments and grimaces. "It turned out to be Dung Tro's last gasp. Two hundred plus nations in the General Assembly passed a resolution condemning him for that attack *and* the one on Mom and Dad's house. He has disappeared amidst rumors that he's trying to flee New York before he is tracked down and arrested."

"I'm coming to be with you until all this is over."

"Oh, please, no, Ben," Gen pleads, her face solemn and unhappy. "I almost died thinking about what might have happened to you. You're safe with Dad and Mom. Please stay with them."

"But I need to be with *you*, Gen."

"No more than I need to be with you, love," Geness says, her voice husky. She looks like she's about to cry again. "But you have to be okay for Lodge if anything happens to me."

"No," I protest. "We all belong together no matter what happens."

"I promise it won't be long," Gen says quietly, ignoring my plea. "Whatever happens is going to happen soon."

"After I milk the cows tonight, I want another chance to talk to you about this," I tell her, sounding for all the world like a pouty teenager whose girlfriend is too busy to spend time with him. "This topic is not closed," I insist.

"I love you, Ben," Gen says ignoring me again. She ends the call without saying goodbye. What the hell?

Totally bummed, I pull up my netacts meds list and pluck an anti-depressant *and* a shot of Valium. That's a heavy dose of feel better. And my suit doesn't veto my request. I feel my collar administer the drugs. All right. I don't feel better. I didn't expect to. I feel numb. And that's *exactly* what I was after.

I walk back to Corkabee's kitchen. She's sitting at the kitchen table watching the wall television. A talking head is reporting on the failed helicopter raid on the White House, but doesn't mention the one that targeted us. Fine. Makes everybody around here feel all the safer I suppose.

Corky sees me and gets up to pour me a fresh cup of coffee. She sets it down on the table next to where she is sitting. I sit there and together we watch the networks endlessly report that Dung Tro has disappeared from UN headquarters in New York City. And that Martian mission commander Gary Friedman has declared that he controls neutron missiles on an orbiting spaceship that can be launched in support of the UN coalition led by Geness.

I glance over at Cork. She obviously finds all of this stuff exciting and, truth be told, so do I. Which actually disturbs me. But there is no escaping the fact that my wild week of life-and-death adventures exposed a streak in my psyche that now craves more such thrills. As much as I hated being dumped into the Potomac, I relished Talbot bashing the turtle's head in. I threw up when I saw her step on Adrian Modigliarty, but watching him die was so intense I would have done anything to get laid that very second. I know that is so screwed up, but there's more.

I loved seeing the jets blow the living shit out of the helicopter pilots coming to kill me. Some part of me actually hopes at this point that Friedman decides to try and liquidate Tro and his supporters, allowing me to cheer the mass extinction of the know-it-all Chinese who are backing him.

So, what kind of man does this new enthusiasm for savagery make me? Someone I hardly recognize, that's for sure. Someone violent and murderous. Once a Jekyll. Now a Hyde. Completely corrupted by my exposure to the first Originals to walk the Earth in five hundred years. As difficult as it is to admit, I wonder if Dung Tro had this all figured out way before anyone else did. Then he chose to risk everything in an effort to destroy the Originals as soon as he learned about their return. If he had succeeded, would he be a hero now instead of a renegade? A messiah who put out fire with fire?

God. This is complicated. But if *I* were supposed to be the One figuring this stuff out, I'd be *Him* instead of me, and that would *not* be a good idea.

What is your plan, Almighty Ben?

Don't have one. It's five o'clock. Time to milk my cows.

CHAPTER 30

"I'm off to the farm," I tell Corkabee. With Stratsen killed there is no one anywhere to help with the chores. Jesus. Stratsen. I forgot about him lying dead on my lawn with a laser hole in his forehead. I tell Corky what happened and ask her to call the folks he worked for. She knew Stratsen and remembers him as a kind soul. That part of him may have leaked out of the back of his head, I'm afraid. Corky agrees to call his employers. She goes off to fetch Wilson in case he needs to tell me anything. He comes to the kitchen and shakes my hand.

"Goodbye," he says rather formally.

"I'm coming back."

"Well, I hope so. I will be anticipating important information when you do."

Wow. That's not the warmest sendoff I've ever received. If Wilson's daughter Geness had gotten his personality, she'd probably still be the president of the United States. She would not, however, be my wife.

"Don't worry," I assure Wilson. "I'll find out if Talbot has a chip. Or at least determine whether she knows if she has one or not."

"You must bring her directly here if she does," he insists. "It's a game changer, Ben. With her help I can neutralize Admiral Friedman, and do it in such a way that neither he nor anyone else will know that his threats of intervention will have been neutralized." Wilson pauses and waits, looking at me as though I may need to have that explained some more.

"I get it," I tell him. "How big is the chip you're looking for?" I ask out of curiosity. Most chips made these days are either big silicon workhorses plugged into electronic circuit boards produced in United Korea and the Three Chinas, or they're skin-thin, impossibly small chips made of organic material like those that function in my netacts. I have no idea what kind of a chip the Martians made and implanted in its space crew, or what one might look like.

Wilson does. "Assuming the chip has a multi-core, integrated circuit capability akin to other devices used in twenty-second century spacecraft that the Martians would use as models, I would guess that it's a silicon sphere about a quarter of an inch in diameter."

"The chip is a sphere?"

"I know. It's crazy old technology," Wilson laughs, amused. "But if Talbot was implanted, that's what she's carrying."

"Okay."

"Explain to her it may have been implanted without her knowledge."

"I got that, Wilson, but Talbot's not some dumb blonde. She'll know exactly why you want that chip."

TALL WAR

Wilson looks insulted.

"Well, of course, she will. I just want her help in defanging Admiral Friedman."

"That's *your* motive. Susan will also know, however, that once you have control of that communication chip you could just as easily send the mother ship back to Mars and launch the missiles at the Lewis and Clark Colony. You're thinking of saving Earth. She'll be thinking of protecting Mars."

"You're absolutely right," Wilson agrees. "The fact is, though, no matter what Astronaut Talbot thinks, the only way for either of us to stop Friedman is to find her chip."

"I'll do the best I can," I promise Wilson. And I will, for in the last analysis he is absolutely right. Retrieving Talbot's chip is the only way for anyone to control Friedman's apocalyptic fever. As I walk back to my farm, I wonder how it came to be that a man of simple pleasures like me—never needing much more than the teats of cow and wife—has been suddenly thrust into the role of savior of the world. I never longed for such a curious and—truth be told—scary responsibility. I have to admit that I have been buzzed by my recent adventures, but as the adrenaline fades I am sure that I will be very glad to change back into Farmer Ben whenever I can.

***

I locate Susan in the woods bordering my farm. It's almost dusk, but I see the smoke from her fire. So much for concealing her presence. I head for the smoke and find that she's roasting a large animal haunch. The rest of the carcass is lying near the fire. It's a deer. Was a deer. Its dead face has the same expression that Stratsen Yun's face did. Who are you?

Talbot sees me approaching.

"Ben!" she cries. "How are you?"

"Got your deer, I see."

She grins proudly.

"Join me for dinner?"

"I can't. I have to milk the cows and my in-laws expect me to return before it gets really late. You could stop by the barn and chat with me when you're done with your dinner."

"I could do that for sure," Susan says amicably. She looks content. She also looks like she has bathed and cleaned up her suit and shoes. She notices me checking her out.

"There's a stream not far from here and a small pond. Bath for me. Scrub-a-dub for the suit. And I'm a new lady."

"You don't need any of that to be a lady," I tell her.

Talbot blushes. Christ Almighty, Katz. Bite your tongue. I leave and walk on down to the smoldering ruins of my home. It was a small place. And it was old. But there were those who loved it. I see worse on my way toward the barn. Helicopter wreckage and human body parts lay strewn about the pasture. Bent rotor blades. A foot in a boot. A head in a helmet. Fire-charred flight cabins with burned torsos strapped into their seats. Arms and legs ripped off and gone.

I search until I find Stratsen's corpse in the backyard grass. Not so far away I find the two agents Talbot tortured and killed. I wonder—not for the first time—how such terrible things can be happening, when only a few days ago no one on Earth including me could have even imagined them?

I cross the yard to the barn. It is the sole surviving reminder that this field of death was once my farm. I open the door and walk in. The interior is softly lit by the last of the afternoon sun's glow and my girls low at me when I enter. I go to the apple bin and scoop up a bucket full of dried Jonathans and pass them out as I greet the cows, telling each one how much I miss her. They seem docile and content, and happy to see me. I dish out the apples, whisper sweet nothings, and watch my girls suck down the fruit.

Man, am I glad to be here. If I were religious, I'd say amen about now.

I settle for shit howdy.

CHAPTER 31

Susan comes by when I'm mostly done with my chores.

"Wow," she says. "This place looks just like the storybooks."

Every cow stops what she is doing and peeks over her divider to get a look at the stranger. Then one by one they begin lowing softly, *mrrrr, mrrr.* Not moo, mind you. Moo is for a kid's books. Real cows go *mrrrr.*

"They like you," I tell Susan.

"You can tell that from the noise they're making?" she asks. I don't think Talbot would admit it, but I can tell she's a little scared.

"They obviously like your voice. Probably like your smell, too."

"My smell?" Talbot says and wrinkles her nose.

"You smell *good*," I clarify.

"Well, at least to the cows," is Susan's comeback.

I'm not touching that. I already stuck my foot in it earlier telling her that I thought she was a lady. I unhook the hose from the shunt I'm holding, then I move to the next pen where I hook it in. Talbot watches me.

"What are you doing?" she asks. I make sure the needle is secure inside the udder shunt and then I explain.

"The hose is connected to a device that sucks the milk from the cows and deposits it directly into pasteurization tanks where it is heated and sterilized. Then it is bottled and stored in refrigeration units, ready for pick-up."

"So, you don't actually milk the cows with your hands?" Susan asks craning her neck to get a closer look at the shunt device.

"No. I'm running a business, not a massage parlor."

Susan laughs loudly. The cows stop their lowing. Susan shakes her head as though she's surprised at her own outburst, but keeps chuckling. I wait for the suction to do its job. The cows begin to *mrrrr* again and I decide this is as good a time as any to start working on Talbot.

"My father-in-law thinks you may be carrying an embedded command chip," I say straight out.

"We talked about this, didn't we, Ben?" Susan says. She is irritated by my question and makes sure that I know it. "Malcolm carried the back-up."

"Yes, but Wilson thinks that if the Mars authorities were concerned about redundant availability, they probably implanted you with one as well."

Susan gets it and grimaces.

"Without informing me."

"Does that really surprise you?" I ask her. "You told me that your purpose on the mission was to take care of Gary. Implanting you with a back-up chip for his use would simply be another way of having you serve his needs. Anyway, that's my thought on the matter for what it's worth."

Susan looks away and doesn't answer. I wonder if she loves Friedman? She left Mars and any family or friends she had in order to be with him. But she's never hinted at how she feels about him.

Susan turns back to me.

"Where would it be?" she asks.

"Wilson thinks it was probably embedded in a fold of muscle where it wouldn't be obvious to you."

Susan is looking at me like she is listening, but I can tell that some part of her brain is trying to figure out *when* the authorities on Mars might have had the opportunity to insert the chip into her body. *And where.* I've been wondering that myself. It is obviously embedded someplace where it doesn't cause Susan any irritation.

I've watched TV documentaries about old timers who carried bullets around in their bodies back in the day that couldn't be removed, so I know Talbot could indeed carry a chip and never be bothered by it. I also figure that it is deliberately implanted in a place where Talbot would have difficulty getting at it. Big nightmare for the Mars' boys if Susan went ballistic and pulled out the chip herself.

"Why is your wife's father interested in whether or not a chip has been implanted on me?" Talbot asks almost nonchalantly. She thinks she's being sly, but I recognize that tone. I use it on cows during inoculation season.

"I think you already know," I say without being defensive.

"Tell me anyway."

Fine. Might as well just say it straight out. Besides, I don't know another way.

TALL WAR

"He thinks he can use it to access your orbiting ship's computers and prevent Gary from launching any of the missiles."

"Not to mention keeping the commander of the expedition from getting word back to Mars about what happened."

"Possibly," I admit. "For now, he just wants to keep Gary from blowing up New York, or Beijing, or wherever Dung Tro is hiding out."

"For now," Susan repeats.

I look into Talbot's questioning eyes.

"For *now* is good, Susan."

Susan looks away again, thinking her own thoughts. I remove the shunt from the last cow, Golda, and my chores are finished. I gather up my equipment and carry it over to the heating tank for sterilization. Talbot watches me. When I'm done, I wash my hands and dry them, then I rub them with an antibacterial lotion. I look at Susan. She looks at me.

"You wanna see if we can find that little fucker?" she asks. "I'll decide later whether it's coming out or not."

"Fine with me," I tell her, concealing how happy her decision makes me. She reaches down and sets me on top of a wooden stall divider. Then she slips off her boots and unzips her suit. She steps out of it and drapes it on the divider next to me. She unfastens her bra. Shucks down her panties. Then she lays them over her suit. She stands naked and unembarrassed. Six feet of gorgeous female.

"Check every inch of my body," she orders. "Don't be shy. And don't be a gentleman. You're looking for *scars*. Describe every single scar. *One of them* I'm not going to remember."

"Come closer," I tell her. "In case I have to poke at something suspicious."

STEPHEN HOUSER

Susan looks at me and arches an eyebrow.
"All right. But no pulling, pinching, or sucking."
I look up at her.
"Not unless you tell me to."
Susan laughs and wags her finger at me.

CHAPTER 32

Susan stands facing me. I take in her naked landscape. Keep in mind that she's an Original-size human and I'm a Final. She is twelve times taller than me. If I were the six-footer, not Talbot, I'd be examining a seventy-two-foot-tall woman. As pleasant as the task of checking out a giant nude woman may sound to you, it's going to take *me* a lot of effort to check out the yards and yards of naked female flesh standing in front of me, so you can shut up.

I search the surfaces of Susan's skin carefully. I don't really see any obvious place to imbed a chip on the front of her body. There are virtually no areas of dense muscle except for her biceps and thighs. She would easily have noticed a new incision in any of those places.

I think for a moment that it's possible that the chip might be imbedded beneath a breast. The incision could be hidden by the line where Susan's breast folds against her chest. But again, I'm sure that a new incision there would have been easy for Susan to spot, not to mention providing a location too easy to get at.

"Could you turn around, please?" I ask her.

Susan does and I am looking straight at her butt. There are multiple curves created by fat deposits, and by sheer good luck my eyes are drawn to where Susan's hips begin to curve toward her buttocks. They are firm areas. Places where a spherical chip could be hidden beneath the soft tissue of the hip yet lodged securely in the large glute muscles underneath.

"Can you stand closer to me?" I ask.

Susan scootches closer. I am only inches away from her lower back and hips. I slowly survey the curves of her hips.

"Your skin is really pale," I tell her. "Guess you never went outside, huh?"

"Well, not for a tan anyway," she explains. "Dumb ass." I grin. She thrusts her hands behind her back. "Check out my tan here," she tells me. Her hands have turned a deep brown from her days in the wilderness, which alerts me to something important I hadn't thought of before.

"Are you right- or left-handed?" I ask.

Susan flexes her right hand.

"Right-handed," she says.

Still one more implant Mission Control precaution, I'm guessing, would have been to put the chip where a right-handed person wouldn't normally reach. I lean close and look at Susan's left hip. And there I find what I'm looking for. A gray-colored scar no thicker than a human hair, located where Susan's hip meets her waist. It looks to be just a tad over a half-inch long. A beautiful job. Almost invisible. Yet I have no doubt what it conceals.

"May I touch your skin?" I ask.

"I said, don't be a gentleman," Susan says irritably. "Do what you need to do."

TALL WAR

I reach out my finger and touch the line. It is definitely a scar. A bit discolored with a tougher texture than the skin on either side of it.

"I have found a small scar. Did you feel my finger?"

"Barely."

"Okay. This time I'm going to push down and see if I can feel the chip beneath your skin and—"

I stop myself from saying *fat*. It's not a word I would use around a naked woman, let alone one as big as a seven-story building. I reach out and press my finger against the scar. The only resistance I feel is Susan's flesh. There is nothing hard like a silicon ball. I push deeper.

"Ow! Watch it, buster," Susan complains. "Are you sure that's just your finger?" She whirls around and glares at me. I am eyeball to outie with Susan's belly and her pubic mound. It is covered with blonde hair. I look up at her and hold my finger up for her to inspect.

"All right," she says, her eyes twinkling mischievously. "Keep going." She turns her back to me again. I push deep against the scar again and all around it. Nothing.

"I can't feel the chip. But I'm sure this is where it has to be," I tell her.

Susan turns around again.

"How can you be so sure? I think you should do my front." She stands with her hands on her hips, breasts thrust out. She tries not to grin, but she does.

"Quit that, please," I say.

Talbot laughs, entertained by her own teasing. She gets dressed and asks me if I'd like to take some deer meat to Wilson and Corkabee.

"No, thanks," I respond. "But I have something for you. The bin at the end of the stalls is filled with dried apples. They're big and they taste good. Help yourself while I put away my stuff."

Susan walks down the wooden plank walkway on the barn floor to the apple bin. I put the hose away. Then I take the needles out of the sterilizer and put them in a chemical bath. Susan walks up munching a puckered-up apple.

"Wow," she says happily.

I nod, and make the pitch I've been working on.

"If you want to come with me to the Wilson's, I am sure we can find a way to get that chip removed tonight."

"I'll come," Susan responds amicably. "But it might only be to ask Wilson some questions."

"Fair enough." I figure getting her to come along is half the battle. "I'm going to grab a couple of things and then I'll be ready."

I head for a supply cabinet at the front of the barn. I open its doors and reach for my personalized first aid kit. I pop the plastic box open and take out a scalpel. Tweezers. Antiseptic salve. Gauze. And medical tape. I put them all in a plastic baggie, then I close up the kit and put it back.

"Do I want to know what you fetched?" Susan asks when I return. Her eyes are fastened on the Ziploc bag in my hand.

I hold it up. She bends down and looks at it.

"State-of-the-art removal devices," I tell her.

"HereHere in your barn?" Susan asks, a doubtful expression on her face.

"Perfect for getting ticks off the cows."

"What's a tick?" Susan asks, standing up again.

"A small, blood-sucking insect."

TALL WAR

"Yuck!" she exclaims. "Do I have any on me?"

"Not that I could see."

"Oh, my God," Susan moans and shudders.

All righty then. Good to see that there's some old-fashioned female beneath all of Talbot's attitude. We head out of the barn. As Susan leaves, the cows *mrrrrr* loudly. I think they've fallen in love.

I can relate. When Susan was standing naked in front of me, I almost went *mrrrrr* myself.

CHAPTER 33

Shock and awe are the only words that can describe Corkabee's face when she opens the door and looks up at Susan Talbot. Everyone has seen Originals in old movies and TV vids, but there isn't a wallscreen big enough anywhere to prepare you for a real one towering over you.

"Hi, Corky," I say. She slowly lowers her gaze until she sees me. "Corkabee Jones, this is Lieutenant Commander Susan Talbot, one of the astronauts from Mars. Susan, this is my wife's mother, Corkabee Wilson."

"Nice to meet you," Susan says.

Corky nods, but stands dazed, completely overwhelmed by the presence of an Original fem on her doorstep.

"Corky, we came to visit with Carmel," I say. She looks at me. I can't tell if she is listening. "Cork?"

She just stares at me.

"Wilson?" I ask.

"I'm sorry," Corkabee mumbles, recovering her manners. "Come in, please."

TALL WAR

We wait in the entry hall while she leaves to get her husband. Talbot looks at the gorgeous house interior and shakes her head in awe. I realize it's her first time seeing anything besides my barn. Susan is as dazzled by the size and wealth of the mansion as poor Corky was by Talbot's size. Moments later Wilson walks into the hall and stops dead when he gets his first sight of Talbot.

"My gosh," he says craning his neck back and looking all the way up at Susan's face. "You are really beautiful."

"Wilson," I say, "this is Martian Astronaut, Lieutenant Commander Susan Talbot. Susan, this is Carmel Wilson, Gen's father."

"Hello," my father-in-law says, a pleased smile on his face. "Please call me Wilson."

"Thank you, Wilson," Talbot replies. "I'd be pleased if you'd call me Susan."

"Okay," Wilson says, plainly star-struck by the six-foot beauty.

I tap him on the shoulder. He ignores me. I look over at Corkabee. Her face looks like she's ready to whack her husband a good one. I tap Wilson's shoulder a little harder.

"What?" he asks, his eyes still riveted on Talbot.

"I'm pretty sure that Susan *is* carrying an embedded command chip, just as you thought. She was not informed that it was going to be implanted. And she has no memory of the procedure. With her permission I found a nearly invisible incision scar at the top of her left hip."

"Well, I suggest that we have some dinner and coffee and talk about possibilities," Wilson says amicably.

"Thank you, but I've eaten," Talbot responds. "And Ben already took care of my sweet tooth back at his place with some delicious apples. If it would be at all possible, however, I would love to have a cup of coffee."

"Listen, honey," Corky says. "I not only have coffee, but I have full-size colonial-era tea cups that you may choose from. You're welcome, in fact, to help yourself to the one used by George Washington. But I'd advise you not to take the one labeled Benjamin Franklin."

Wilson and I chuckle. Susan looks at Corkabee for an explanation.

"Franklin was a bit of a ladies' man," she explains. "Can't be sure just where his lips might have been." Wilson chuckles.

"Good one, Corky," he says, looking at his wife admiringly.

Corkabee directs Wilson and me to bring the kitchen table and chairs over to the colonial dining table where Susan handily moves them on top of the Original-size table. She sits in one of the old, waxed hickory chairs and watches while Corky sets the small table. Then Corky makes multiple pots of coffee, slowly filling up an old bone China tea cup from England.

Susan is invited to add milk and sugar, but she takes it black. Which is good, I figure, as I doubt very much that there is enough of either one of those in the house to affect Susan's coffee. Talbot drinks her coffee while Cork serves Wilson and me dinner. I dig into the pulled pork, scalloped potatoes, and fresh corn-on-the-cob, while Susan diplomatically—but thoroughly—questions Wilson on what he thinks he would do if he had one of the Martian communication chips in his hands. He answers her frankly, and probes Talbot in return, trying to get her to remember what she can about the orbiting spaceship's computers and missile system applications.

TALL WAR

Corkabee serves me seconds and I don't say no. She cooked the pork for hours and it is tender and tasty. Corky also fills my wine glass more than once and I drink it all. I usually prefer a good whup of Valium to the slower down of alcohol. Tonight, however, I am witnessing something I want to remember and I drink to mark the occasion.

It is a truly pivotal moment for the future of the human race. Not to mention the fate of the four of us sitting at this table, as Susan listens to Wilson's reasons for denying Gary Friedman's unchecked access to the *Kennedy's* arsenal of missiles. I eat my food and sip my wine and watch the lengthy and detailed back-and-forth between Talbot and Wilson. Then there is a shift in the kinds of questions Talbot is asking. I know in my heart that Wilson has made a breakthrough.

"How would you remove the chip?" she asks him.

"I have a local anesthetic that will numb the skin and the muscle beneath the scar to the depth of three centimeters or so. Ben will sterilize and use the small scalpel you saw to make an incision and retrieve the chip. He'll close the incision with a laser and protect it with and antiseptic cream, sterile gauze, and tape. You might feel a little tenderness afterwards, but nothing more."

"What will happen to me after the chip is removed?" she asks.

"I would guess you'll be a hero," Wilson responds. "All over the world."

"And you'll probably be asked to join the United Nations as an ambassador for the colonists on Mars," I add.

"Best of all," Corkabee jumps in, "Gary will get his priorities straightened out. You two will get married and have babies." Corky smiles, deeply emotional at the thought of love triumphing.

Susan laughs and shakes her head.

"All right," she says. "No one's going to be able to top Corkabee. Let's get the chip out."

I look at Corky. What do you say to someone who just saved the world? She smiles happily.

"Excellent," Wilson says beaming.

"You can use the Adams Bedroom," Corkabee tells him.

"Will there be much blood?" Susan asks, not afraid, but curious.

"Very little," Wilson answers her. "But we'll be prepared just in case."

"All right," Talbot responds. "But nothing's going to happen until all the dishes are washed up, and *you boys are helping*."

Corky grins and Wilson and I start clearing the table. While it doesn't exactly feel like a call to action to save a world in peril, I don't mind. We all need a splash of normalcy in a day full of craziness, *and* it will provide a bit of color when I record this on some future wiki.

Wilson helps Corky wash the dishes and I dry. When we're finished, we'll walk down to the Adams Bedroom with Martian Astronaut Susan Talbot who is prepared to offer her naked backside to my scalpel to save the planet.

Just another day in the life of a Virginia dairyman.

CHAPTER 34

The Adams Bedroom is majestic, decorated with beautiful maple furniture fashionable a thousand years ago. There is a colonial four-poster bed with white curtains and a lovely flower-print sofa with end tables. If President John Adams really did stay here, it was a lovely place to take his rest. And the memory of his visit proudly abides in folktales as a bit of period nostalgia. But as for real history? That's what we're about to make now.

I put a stack of bath towels on the bed and set down the thermos full of alcohol holding my sterilized scalpel and tweezers. I boiled both instruments for half an hour and transferred them directly to the thermos bottle. Corkabee brings several large pots of boiling water and hand towels, plus a bowl full of cotton balls in case blood becomes an issue.

Susan spreads out the bath towels on the bed. Then she unzips her flight suit, pulls it off, and lies face down on the bed. I ask her to pull the left side of her underpants down. She does, revealing her hip and buttock. I apologize and ask permission for Wilson and me to stand on Talbot's back. I locate the scar at her hip immediately and point it out to Wilson.

He bends over and studies it, then tells me that it is very much the size and type of scar that would result from a procedure to implant the chip. I repeat his words to Susan, who nods. I swab the area with the disinfecting anesthetic Wilson hands me. After a moment I use a syringe to inject a pain killer into the tissue underneath and wait for it to take effect.

"Do you want to know when we're done?" I call to Susan.

"I want to know when you *start*," she calls back, "when you *finish*, and everything in between."

I clench my teeth so no rude words can escape. The big girl is a wus.

"Fine," I manage to mutter. Then I speak loud enough for Talbot to hear. "I have applied an anesthetic to your skin and administered a numbing agent into the flesh. It will take effect in a minute or two."

I look at Susan's white skin. I suspect that it has probably never been exposed to the sun. It has, however, been exposed to someone's scalpel. I focus on the scar left by their tampering. I take the lid off the alcohol-filled thermos and take out my own scalpel.

"I am going to make a very small incision," I warn Susan. "I guarantee that you will not feel a thing." I touch the tip of the scalpel exactly on the top of Susan's scar. Then I push down ever so slightly. The blade dips into Talbot's flesh and a drop of blood seeps out. But only a drop. I slowly slice along the scar. Susan lies silent and unmoving. Wilson watches, completely still. A bit more blood flows out. Since I am only navigating through Talbot's body fat, I ignore it and cut deeper until I have gone down about an inch through the skin and fat, and into the muscle below. I put the scalpel down.

"Feel anything?" I ask Susan.

"No," she says.

"Want some lipo while I'm down here?" I ask.

"That better be a joke," Susan threatens.

"Wilson made me ask," I lie. He grins and shakes his finger at me. "I'm going to probe for the chip now," I say.

"Go ahead. Tell me when you find it."

I reach my hand inside the wound and find the silicon implant right away, lurking at the bottom of my incision.

"I've got it," I tell Susan. "It's about the size of a pea in your terms. Close to a cantaloupe in ours."

"A cantaloupe?" Susan groans instantly worried. "How are you going to get that out?"

"Like this," I say and put both of my hands inside the opening. Wilson's eyes grow big, but before he can lecture me on proper hygiene I have the silicon sphere out. It's bloody and I set it down on the towel.

"Feel anything?" I call out to Susan.

"Not a thing," she answers.

"Well, it's out. Congratulations. Now I'm going to finish up."

"Will I feel that?"

"Don't think so. You might get a whiff of burning flesh when I use the laser to cauterize the wound."

"Oh, Lord," Susan groans.

"I thought you were an atheist," I say, using a cotton puff to dab blood away from the cut.

"Oh, yeah. I forgot," Susan says. "How about shit howdy?"

"Always works for me."

I motion Wilson to pinch the skin together, showing him with my fingers what I want him to do. He pinches the surgical wound closed quite precisely. I run the tip of the laser down the incision and in moments it is closed. I swab an antibiotic ointment on the skin and tape gauze over it.

"All done," I tell Susan.

"May I sit up?"

"Yes. And you can have the first look at your baby."

Susan rolls over and sits up on the edge of the mattress. Wilson wipes the chip off with a hand towel and holds the small silver globe out for Susan to see. She touches it with her fingertip.

"Son of a bitch," she growls. She glances at me, her face etched with fury. "Gary knew, didn't he?"

I don't answer. I mean, I didn't really know, did I?

Wilson unfortunately tries to put some lipstick on the pig.

"Maybe the admiral had specific orders to keep its presence secret," he suggests.

"Think so?" Susan sneers at him. "Well, whether he did or did not, I can tell you it's going to be a long time before he gets his dick sucked again."

Wilson looks like he's going to have an aneurism. I take it in stride having been exposed to Talbot's suggestive vocabulary. Both Wilson and I stare at Susan, long bare legs crossed, breasts overflowing her bra. She looks at us.

"Why are you two just standing there?" she demands.

Well, the truth of the matter is that I am not going anywhere with a hard-on. I look over at Wilson. He's staying put, too.

I start laughing. So does he.

Susan sits there watching us. Frowning. Wondering what the hell our problem is.

TALL WAR

I'm not telling.

Wilson wipes the perspiration off his forehead with a handkerchief.

He's not telling either.

CHAPTER 35

Wilson disappears with the command chip. Susan dresses while I clean up. Then Corky is kind enough to serve all of us coffee in the kitchen. We watch the television wallscreen on the kitchen wall. The United Nations General Assembly has passed a resolution condemning Dung Tro for abuse of powers, stripped him of his office as president of the Security Council, and banned his presence from all UN properties and facilities worldwide. Tro, however, has been absent and unaccounted for since late last night.

Immediately after that story a vid plays showing the United States' new UN delegate, Carroll Harry Lee, appearing live before the General Assembly. The announcer reports that Mr. Lee is standing in for America's permanent delegate, Rigging Nash. Where is *that* bastard, I wonder? In hiding learning Chinese?

Carroll Harry Lee reads a prepared message declaring that the US federal government intends to file criminal charges against Dung Tro with the World Court in The Hague, and with the

TALL WAR

First District Court in New York City. Charging him with the murder of Spaceman Malcolm Saint Jean and holding him responsible for multiple homicides in the deaths of the soldiers and pilots ordered to attack the president's White House home.

Lee is cut off mid-sentence by an announcer with breaking news from Beijing. Cameras show Dung Tro addressing a giant throng of supporters in Tiananmen Square. There are cheers as he speaks. The crowd is loud and vehement. Though Tro is speaking Mandarin, the announcer instantly translates Tro's words into English. Tro's handsome face is angry. His eyes flash with indignation.

"I have returned to Beijing after being treated shamefully by the Western powers that control the UN." (There are boos and hisses from the crowd.) "My name and my reputation have been dishonored." (More boos and hisses.) "But every word I uttered as president of the Security Council, and every deed I performed in that office was done on behalf of the people of the *entire* world." (Whistling and cheering.)

"All my efforts were directed at trying to prevent the destruction that is now being threatened by the alien, Gary Friedman." (Screams and cries.) "The Originals passed this world to the Finals." Tro holds his arms wide. "And they made no provision whatsoever for sharing it with anyone, ever." (Shouts and hoorays.) "Certainly not with Martian Originals *who were banned from returning to Earth half a millennium ago.*" (Wild cheering.)

"Effective immediately, the Beijing government has authorized me to prepare the army, the navy, and the air force for action against the United States, unless it acts immediately to imprison Martian Astronauts Gary Friedman and Susan Talbot and try them on charges of spying on the Earth in order to prepare for a Martian invasion." (Hysterical shouting.) Dung Tro bows and then exits the stage. (Cheering continues on and on.)

Tro's words are everything but an official declaration of war. A commentator analyzing the speech announces that all of the United Nations' forces deployed in the capitals of the Three Chinas—Beijing, Hong Kong, and Shanghai—have been expelled.

Corkabee and Susan stay glued to the television. I decide to check on Wilson. He's been on his own for a couple of hours now and I'm curious as to whether any of his hopeful thoughts about cracking the chip's codes still look doable now that he's actually had it in his hands for a while.

I excuse myself and walk back down to Wilson's workplace. The door is open, but the room is darker than usual. The overflowing shelves and tables suddenly look ominous and threatening. Even the dozens of computer monitors and screens—usually bright with vids and colorful stats—have gone black.

I carefully follow the aisle to Wilson's desk. I am unnerved by the mountain of clutter everywhere. I calm myself down by imagining what it would be like for Wilson to walk into *my* work area. A huge barn filled with giant cows. And giant crap.

Wilson is seated at his desk, staring at a single lit up monitor displaying a variety of word combinations drawn from a single set of letters listed on the screen. Anagrams. What is he searching for?

"Hello," I say softly.

"Oh. Hi, Ben," Wilson answers without looking away from his screen.

"How are you doing?" I ask.

"Great, actually. I was able to add myself as a user to the communication chip and remotely logged into the *Kennedy's* onboard computers. I was able to hack into the encrypted root passwords for the missile programs. I changed Friedman's user ID and password and replaced them with my own. Now I'm testing anagrams of Gary's old codes to see if he stored any variations as back-ups."

Of course. What else would you do?

"Could you tell whether Gary has actually used his own chip to access the spaceship's computers?"

"It appears that he has not," Wilson answers slowly. "There were no records of log-ins, or attempted log-ins, before or since the *Kennedy* was placed in Earth orbit and the space capsule deployed. Which not only means that Friedman has not attempted to enter the ship's computers, but Rigging Nash's agents apparently got no further than reading a list of the programs active on the *Jon Jon*."

That's all good news. No one has fiddled with the *Kennedy's* computers except for Wilson. And if Admiral Friedman is really serious about directing the spaceship's missiles toward Earth, Wilson has locked him out. Even if the commander can still access the ship's computer with his own chip, I doubt Gary has the technical skill to undo the new encrypted ID and passwords that Wilson has installed. Of course, there is always the possibility that Mission Control on Mars can help Gary regain control of the weapon systems. But for now, our world is not a sitting duck.

"Let's call Gen and tell her the news," Wilson says enthusiastically. He uses a secure line and looks at me while he waits for her to pick up. He nods toward the large monitor sitting on the table. It lights up as Geness answers. I can see that she is still in the Oval Office. The girl works longer hours than a dairyman. Wilson points at a webcam attached to the upper corner of the monitor and motions me closer. Gen's eyes light up when she sees me.

"Hello, love," she says. "How are you?"

"Fine," I tell her a little stiffly. I still feel stung by how she treated me the last time we talked.

"We're both fine," Wilson says crowding in next to me. "How are *you* holding up, dear?"

"Good," she replies. "Everything seems to be moving at lightning speed here. Dung Tro has been booted from the UN, but all Three Chinas have declared political and military loyalty to that snake, and they're ready to risk war."

"But not on Tro's behalf," Wilson says. "They are gearing up to destroy the Martian spacemen."

"Yes," Gen says. "Our whole world seems to have gone to hell in a hand basket ever since that damn space capsule landed in the Potomac. As much as Dung Tro overstepped his authority, I can relate to the fear and panic gripping the Earth. I can't think of a single good thing that will come out of the Martin Originals' return. Not now. Not later. They didn't do themselves any favors carting nukes down here either."

"All true, Gen," Wilson agrees. "But I think it fair to remember that the Martians haven't actually caused any trouble yet. In fact, Gary Friedman has been a very public supporter of yours."

Gen shakes her head.

"Dad, I appreciate your perspectives, but my panicked constituency is not going to allow me to take the high road here. Please tell me you were able to take control of the spaceship's missiles and maybe I can tone down my pissiness." Gen waits.

"I was."

"Yes!" she exclaims. "Tell me everything."

TALL WAR

Wilson proceeds to explain his activities worming his way through the orbiting ship's computer programs. Carmel's technical talk is voodoo to me, but it's obvious that he has saved the day, Gen's day, my day, and the whole damn world's day.

Corkabee sticks her head in the far doorway and calls to Wilson.

"What?" he calls back.

"You'd better come," Corky tells him, her voice urgent. "Gary Friedman is going to appear live on the networks."

"Why?"

"No one knows. He requested an opportunity to speak. News commentators are predicting that he's going to demand that the Beijingers turn Dung Tro over to the World Court."

"And if they don't?"

"Who knows?" Corky snaps. "Why do you think we're glued to the TV?"

I hope Gen has talked to Gary. If he's acting on his own, then not only will we have Washington and China facing off over Dung Tro, but we'll also have Admiral Gary Friedman in the mix as a wild card. 'Course he doesn't know that he's been hung out to dry by Wilson and has no missiles to play with.

Ain't we got fun?

CHAPTER 36

Wilson and I follow Corky back to the kitchen just in time to see Gary Friedman appear on the TV screen. He is standing behind an acrylic podium with a single microphone. He is wearing a plain, silver flight suit without any decoration. His movie-star face is clean shaven and his hair is Hollywood perfect. In fact, the admiral is holding himself as if he's *playing* a space hero. His face is deadly serious. I glance over at Susan. She's just as sober-faced as he is.

The spaceship captain begins to read from a prepared script placed on the podium. Gary looks at it from time to time, but maintains strong eye contact with the cameras carrying his image to the millions of people who are seeing and hearing him for the first time. The effect is powerful. I am sure Gary knows that and counts on it.

"Brothers and sisters of Earth," he begins. "My name is Gary Friedman and I'm from Nashville, Tennessee."

Good God. I didn't expect that. I glance at Wilson and Corkabee. They look as stunned as I am. Susan looks guarded, as though Gary has just begun an act that only she will be able to see through.

"I am an Earthman from Mars," Friedman continues. "An American from the Lewis and Clark Colony started by the United States of America five hundred years ago." Gary's face looks calm and peaceful, as if he were addressing long lost relatives he has now thankfully been reunited with. Nice job, Gary.

"For the first century and a half of the Earth's colonization efforts on Mars, our relationship flourished. Until the people of Earth—in the throes of a total ecological crisis—focused their last energies on trying to survive the imminent death of the doomed planet and ended all contact with the Earth colonists on Mars. Maintaining a fervent hope in our hearts that someday we might be able to return to our home planet, we labored alone on Mars for centuries, growing and prospering, but always praying for the day when we would be able to build spaceships of our own and travel to Earth."

I shouldn't believe that, but I do. Susan told me that Gary's father was very religious. Why shouldn't his son be? And maybe he genuinely is. Just like Cortes. Conquer. Kill. Pray. Maybe pray should be listed first.

"That day came in my lifetime," Friedman says, his eyes moist, I swear. "I and my crew are the first Americans from Mars to return in 500 years. First Officer Malcolm Saint Jean. Communications Officer Susan Talbot. And me, the ship's captain, Gary David Friedman, landed here exactly seven days ago.

"We were greeted graciously by United Nations' General Weldon Wainwright, President Geness Jones of the United States, and a group of Earth leaders who not only made us feel welcome, but immediately began to provide us with fresh provisions. Our initial contact was completely devoid of suspicion or fear on anyone's part, despite the fact that my crew and I were Original-size humans and the people of the United States were Final-size humans. Together, the beneficiaries of Mars' colonization and the Downsizing effort that saved the Earth's people."

This guy is smooth. He is demonstrating all the charming traits that won me over at the get go, just as he is surely winning over any critics in his vast television audience who tuned in expecting to see a madman from Mars. Gary looks up from his prepared remarks and speaks earnestly to the cameras.

"Unknown, however, to the leaders who welcomed us, secret unauthorized orders to assassinate me and my crew had been drafted by Dung Tro, the president of the United Nations Security Council. We know this to be true from Tro's private communications, which were intercepted and released for the whole world to see.

"Sadly, his murderous plotting was uncovered only after his agents had succeeded in blowing up our space capsule and killing Spaceman Saint Jean. The explosion that destroyed our ship also blew Officer Talbot into the Potomac River and threw me off the capsule's landing platform constructed by UN engineers.

"Also, one of the saddest moments of that terrible hour was the disappearance of Benedict Katz, the husband of President Jones, who had headed up the food program to aid me and my crew. Thank God, both he and Susan Talbot actually survived and are alive today." Gary shakes his head modestly, as though marveling at the goodness of God. Or the quirky circumstances of fate. Take your choice. Either way, his affectation melts my heart.

"The people of Earth also know that when Dung Tro found out that these two missing heroes had, in fact, been found alive," Gary continues his voice tense and urgent, "he ordered his agents to track them down and kill them." Friedman pauses dramatically. "He also ordered an attack on the White House in Washington, DC, to assassinate President Jones.

"These heinous and despicable actions were thwarted by defensive military actions courageously conducted by General Wainwright. Dung Tro's activities have been condemned by the United Nations Security Council and General Assembly. But that architect of death has fled to Beijing, where not only has that Chinese government offered him sanctuary, but all Three Chinas have declared their intention to go to war against the United States unless both Susan Talbot and I are arrested and forbidden from interacting with the good people of Earth."

Gary has been restrained and articulate. He has summarized the issues facing him and the nations of the world. The question now, is what does he propose to do about them? Friedman reaches down and picks up his speech again. He narrows his eyes, and in serious, even daunting tones, reads verbatim from his prepared remarks. What he has to say will rock the foundations of our civilization.

"As of four o'clock this afternoon," he begins, "North American Eastern Time, I have activated twenty-four ballistic missiles on the orbiting mother ship that brought me and my crew here. Three of these missiles are now in a timed launch mode. Their targets are Beijing, Shanghai, and Hong Kong. This was not done to threaten the people of those great cities, but rather to force the authorities in those domains to arrest Dung Tro and surrender him to United Nations officials."

Gary pauses and looks directly at the camera for a long moment. His is not the face of a man playing out a bluff. It is a hard and ruthless face that will carry out exactly what he has threatened.

I just hope the goddamn Chinese and can see that for themselves. This isn't fucking Mahjong.

Gary goes back to his script.

"If my warning is not heeded, exactly twenty-four hours from now launch countdowns will automatically begin on the orbiting Martian craft. The missiles—each bearing a neutron warhead—will be fired. The populations of China's greatest cities will be erased from the globe."

Gary puts down his papers again and talks to the world.

"My decision is non-negotiable. There is too much at risk, and global war is too close at hand for me to stand by and watch one self-deluded man destroy not only Earth's relations with its returning kin from Mars, but plunge this beautiful world into a catastrophic war as well." Friedman softens his voice, and in an emotional voice makes his last appeal.

"Fellow citizens of Earth, I ask that you join me in beseeching God Almighty to open the hearts of the Chinese leaders. That they might lay down their instruments of war and present Dung Tro for the judgment he has brought upon himself. May you and yours be safe. And may we co-exist peacefully together, Earthmen all."

With that Gary bows his head one brief moment, as if he is the first person to pray for the divine intervention he has so fervently urged. Then he turns and leaves the podium. The moment he is gone the talking heads on television literally begin a countdown to the launching of the missiles, calling the twenty-four hours allotted for Dung Tro's arrest a "window of opportunity," a "time of reconciliation," and other bullshit names.

TALL WAR

Jesus, people. Wake up. You're being conned by one of the best. In a single stroke the man from Mars has taken back what billions of Originals died to give us. Namely a world that only a few days ago belonged to six-inch farmers. Now it's in the hands of a six-foot conquistador.

I look at Susan. She's quiet, watching the television commentators spin Gary's speech. Corkabee is standing stunned and silent. Only Wilson shows any life, getting up and walking back to his lab. I run after him.

"I thought you said that Friedman hadn't accessed the missile software?" I tell him.

Wilson stops and turns to face me.

"I told you that I had found no *evidence* of his activity," he refutes me sternly. "I also told you that to prevent any future interface with the Kennedy's computers, I voided Admiral Friedman's user ID and password and searched for any hidden back-ups he may have had. If he has managed to get at the missile systems anyway, then he used a secret method—some kind of secret backdoor to the missile software if you will—that I don't know about."

Holy shit. Why didn't Wilson mention that possibility when he was rambling on about how he had so cleverly robbed Gary of his missiles? Geek oversight? Like holes in your socks? Except more lethal.

"But you can find that secret method, right?" I ask, stoked now with genuine anxiety.

"If anyone can, I can," Wilson says calmly.

"Is that a yes or a no?" I ask, my worry skyrocketing.

"It's a strong maybe."

A strong maybe? My RediMedi shoots me with a slug of Valium without my even having to ask.

"And what if you can't find it?" I ask. Now my fear is going nova.

"I can undo Friedman's commands," Wilson assures me. "Including any timed launches of the missiles. But that won't stop him from doing it again."

Okay. I am calmed a bit. But that may only be the Valium.

"So, it's going to be good versus evil right to the last second?" I moan.

"More like cat and mouse," Wilson answers. "With neither one of us sure where the cat or the mouse is."

I am not comforted by Wilson's analogy. Who's the cat? Who's the mouse? He gazes at me as though waiting for yet another question. I don't have any this particular nanosecond. Wilson can see that and heads down to his lab. I return to the kitchen. Numb enough to spend the rest of the evening watching news vids until I am tired out of my head. I miss Gen terribly, but I decide not to bother her in the middle of the crisis that Gary has stirred up. If she needs anybody, it's going to be Wilson.

That seems ominously like the first letters on the wall spelling doom for our relationship. But like the ruler in the Bible who ignored that warning, I refuse to think of how far away my wife is from wanting me by her side. Instead, I do what any man facing the loss of his true love would do.

I tell my RediMedi to pop me an additional dose of Valium.

My suit nixes the request. Pissed, I pull up the RediMedi meds menu manually, use my netacts curser to underscore the drug, and order it again. My suit turns me down again. Oh, man. Too many missiles and too few drugs. It's clearly going to be one of those nights.

CHAPTER 37

Someone is shaking my shoulder.

"Gen?"

"It's Wilson," my father-in-law whispers. "Sorry to wake you. Gary Friedman has been shot."

I sit up on the bed. Wilson turns the bedside lamp on. I don't remember falling asleep, but I do remember lying down anxious and worried about losing Geness. Wilson sits down on the bed next to me. He looks like hell.

"What happened?"

"Someone attacked the admiral."

"Someone?" I almost shriek. "Someone who?"

Wilson shrugs helplessly.

"No one knows. The rumors are that a group of masked individuals with laser pistols and some kind of stun grenades ambushed him and the UN agents escorting him after his speech last night. Authorities figure they were after whatever device he used to access the spaceship."

I stare at Wilson. Right after Gary announced that he had programmed some of the missiles on the orbiting Martian ship for launch, someone tried to take whatever control mechanism Gary had used to access his spaceship. They couldn't know that he had used a chip. Only Wilson, Gen, and I know about that. Plus, of course, Talbot and Friedman. Yet to attack Gary suggests that his assailants were counting on the fact that he had the control device on his person. Did he? Did they get it? I feel like I've been punched in the stomach.

Wilson gives me some more detail.

"Friedman had left the news studio in Georgetown where he had delivered his speech, walking to a government car scheduled to take him to the Smithsonian where Geness had him lodged in the Lincoln Bedroom from the original White House. He was being escorted by several UN security agents. They were massacred and Friedman was shot and left for dead."

"What about the chip?" I cry. "Did they get the chip?" I know that sounds heartless, but it matters a whole lot more than Gary at this point.

"No one is saying."

"If the Chinese have the chip—"

Wilson interrupts me, "We don't know that the attackers were Chinese."

I scowl at Wilson and finish my question.

"If the Chinese have the chip will they be able to take control of the missiles?"

"They can probably do anything I can do."

That sets me back. I have never, ever heard Wilson say anything like that before.

"Does that make you nervous?" I cry.

TALL WAR

"No," he says simply. "But it does put on more pressure to find out how Friedman accessed the weapons' application. I still can't find any evidence that he even *logged* into the ship's computers, let alone managed to program three missiles. On the other hand, his press conference may have been an elaborate charade after he discovered that his access to the vessel's computer systems had been blocked. The most likely scenario, however—and by far the worst one as I warned you earlier—is that he used a backdoor into the software that only he knew about and accessed the missile software to set the time-delayed commands to launch."

"And you can't find that backdoor?"

"It's almost impossible. In millions of lines of code there would be only one place where he entered. The only good news—short of the miraculous discovery of Friedman's secret backdoor—is that I think I can reprogram the ship to return to Mars. Or maybe more intelligently, fly it into the sun."

I start to jump on that bandwagon. But the moment I open my mouth, Wilson holds his hand up to stop me.

"I can't make that decision. Only the United Nations should do that."

"Send it into the sun, Wilson! It's a war machine with destructive neutron weapons. It has to be destroyed. There isn't a single reason to save it, not one!"

"I agree, Ben. But if I do it on my own authority, then I'm no better than Dung Tro, or Gary Friedman. Making decisions for the whole world."

"Really?" I say, frustrated and raising my voice. "Well, there's a big difference between bad decisions and good decisions."

Wilson nods, but he doesn't answer.

"What time is it?" I ask, still upset, but deflating now like a bike tire with a nail in it. Wilson is more mature than me. I grudgingly give him that. I'd fly that son of a bitch Martian ship into the sun in a heartbeat.

"A little after five in the morning," Wilson says.

"I need to go to the farm and take care of my cows. Did you tell Talbot about the attack on Gary Friedman?"

"No. She left a long time ago. She said she'd meet you at the farm. I've noticed that you two seem close," he says, quietly. "Would you be willing to tell her what happened to Gary?"

"I can do that."

"Thank you, Ben. Tell her that he is in a coma in a government hospital." Wilson stands up. He's wearing an old robe and his bedroom slippers. "Would you like to have some coffee?" he asks.

"Yes."

"Corkabee has been plying me with Java all night long. I'm sure there's a fresh pot in the kitchen."

"Thank you."

Wilson smiles then shuffles off to his workstation, the only hope of humankind. I go find the bathroom thinking of how to break the terrible news to Talbot that Gary has been shot and is in a coma. I can't imagine how you'd feel hearing that your lover is dying. Oddly, it steels my resolve not to let Gen slip through my fingers by letting her get used to me being far away. Tonight, safe or not, I am going to the White House to reclaim my wife.

CHAPTER 38

I use the bathroom then walk down to the kitchen. My stomach is in knots. My head in an uproar. Everything is getting worse and I can't imagine how that's even possible. Friedman is out of it, and his all-powerful communication chip is unaccounted for. Before he was attacked, Gary told the whole world that he had programmed three missiles for launch against China from the orbiting Martian spaceship. If he has indeed done that, the bombs will wipe out everyone living in Beijing, Shanghai, and Hong Kong.

My own woes include that my house is gone. My farm is littered with dead bodies and helicopter wreckage. And I've been separated from my wife and son for a week. I tell my RediMedi to give me something to get my mind off these things. I expect Valium, but my Puritan suit scores me some aspirin. Piss. Shit. Fuck. Pardon my English.

Cork is watching the wallscreen when I come in. She gets up without my asking and pours me some coffee.

"What's happening?" I ask her, though the only news I really care about right now is what Wilson is trying to do in his lab.

"They're about to show security videos of the attack on Admiral Friedman," Corky says, totally stressed out.

"What?" I cry out. I stare at the wallscreen.

"Surveillance cameras caught the whole thing and all the public networks have received a copy."

Right now, a talking head is telling viewers that the Chinese are already denying involvement in the attack on the admiral. Corky brings over a tray with coffees for both of us and the sugar bowl for me. She puts it on the table and sits. The TV head introduces one of the three security videos filmed by cameras mounted on Georgetown buildings in the vicinity of the attack.

The television network rolls the initial surveillance footage on Gary. The picture is green and grainy, obviously recorded at night by an infrared lens. Detail is poor, but there is no doubt that I am seeing Gary Friedman walking tall with several Final UN agents. These forces are elite soldiers from the UN, wearing signature blue berets and carrying laser pistols and rifles.

Suddenly one of the soldiers in front of the detail sprints ahead, spins around to face his colleagues, levels his automatic rifle, and shoots the soldiers. Gary falls backwards, shot as well.

The murderous traitor runs toward Gary. The admiral tries to sit up but falls back. The blue beret pulls himself up onto Friedman's uniform, runs up Gary's chest, and shoots him once in the forehead. Gary never uttered a sound. He lies still.

Cork gasps and covers her mouth. I stare at her. She shakes her head and points at the screen. The assassin pats down Gary's flight suit. It is obvious that Friedman was smart enough not to have carried the communications device on his person. The shooter turns and flees.

I get a brief look at the murderer's face when the television freezes his image. He's not Chinese. He's a goddamn Caucasian, and I would bet the farm that he's another agent of Rigging Nash. I feel humiliated that he could have gotten away with taking Gary down in the middle of the nation's capital.

Corky sits forlorn and looks at me. If it's possible, she looks even more exhausted than Wilson. Wrinkles cover her forehead and deep lines crease the skin under her eyes. Her distraught expression tells me that she is overwhelmed by the terrible video, and she should be. No one in hundreds of years has seen a man shot in cold blood by another human.

Even watching the news stories after the *Jon Jon* was blown up was inadequate preparation for seeing the UN soldiers murdered in cold blood and Gary Friedman drilled right in the forehead. I have nothing to say to Cork. When there's this much blood, how can there be any hope?

I thank her for the coffee, turn down her offer to make me breakfast, and head out the door. I think about the trouble the whole world is in as I walk back to my farm. If Gary was bluffing about arming and aiming the nukes, then four thirty will come and go this afternoon and no one will wind up dead. If he wasn't, then a lot more people are going to die.

It's light out by the time I get to the farm. I try not to look at the charred pile of wood that was my house. Or the twisted metal wrecks and stinking piles of flesh that once made up a fleet of war choppers and young pilots. I focus on my barn. Then on my cows. They are very happy to see me. There is, however, a bit of tentativeness to their lowing. *Mrrrr?* Is it fear stemming from all the violence they heard? No. It's more like a faint longing. Something tells me they're asking about the big girl. *Mrrrr, mrrrr?*

I chat with the ladies and take my time doing the milking. I fill up each cow's feedbox with hay, oats, and some dried apples. When I finish, I feel an overwhelming desire to go into my house and make some coffee. Can't today. But some day in the future I will. Someone is going to fix my house and I'll be drinking all the coffee I want.

> *Dear Dung Tro,*
>
> *Please send a check to pay for rebuilding my house and replacing the furnishings that your agents burned up. ASAP would be nice.*
>
> *You should also send money to cover Stratsen Yun's funeral service, and Gary Friedman's hospital bills.*

I picture Gary's forehead with the laser hole drilled into it. Even if the Chinese capitals do get blown south in a few hours, I refuse to think of Friedman as a bad guy. No, I haven't forgotten Susan's contention that he is a conquistador at heart. But if I think about that I'll just get confused. So, I do what I came to do. I milk. Don't have to think. Don't have to fret. Just have to tend to my cows and everything will be fine.

Plus, we'll all get milk.

CHAPTER 39

It's light out as I leave the dairy barn. I can smell something cooking in the woods. It's got to be Talbot, Virginia's only neutron gun sports enthusiast. Sure enough, following the smell, I find her roasting meat on a barbeque rack. It smells like pork. Did she bag one of the wild boars that run in these forests? I walk right up to the fire where Susan is sitting before she notices me.

"Hey, Ben," she says. She reaches down her hand and lifts me onto her thigh. "How about something to eat?"

"Won't say no," I tell her. "Did you neutronize a boar?"

Susan grins and cuts me off a piece.

"Tell me if it tastes like bacon," she says.

The meat is grayish-brown and doesn't look particularly appetizing. It smells good, though. I pull off a shred and stick it in my mouth.

"Better than bacon," I say surprised. "More like pork tenderloin."

"What's that?"

"Steak. But from a pig. In this case a boar."

I hold out my hand for more.

"Okay, then," Susan replies happily filling it up.

"Nice shooting," I tell her, eating more.

She nods.

"I had to shoot something."

"For Gary?" I ask quietly.

Susan's face crumbles and the tears gush.

"I saw the vids at the Wilson's house," she gasps. "I saw him shot." She cries hard for a while. Then she sighs and stops.

"Maybe he will recover," I say hopefully. "No one has announced that the shot that hit him was fatal."

"You haven't seen any news reporting him dead?" she asks and wipes the tears from her eyes.

"I think you should plan on him recovering. Best way to wait and see. Plan on telling him that it's time to get married, just like Corky said. No more of this slam, bam, thanks for everything, ma'am, crap."

"Get over yourself," Susan says, but smiles.

"I mean it," I insist. "Married. As soon as he recovers. Then kids."

"Whoa," Susan replies. "Let me get the first knot tied. Then I'll work on the next."

"What did you say?" I ask. I have no idea what Talbot meant.

"It's just an old Colony expression."

"Meaning what?" I ask.

"Let me explain," Susan responds. "Martians are practical. With survivor's work ethics. The first colonists worked hard and worked smart, believing that it never paid off to skip steps. They labored to do everything right the first time. Five hundred years later, we're still just as careful to get things done right as they were. Every minute. Every time. Hence, the expression, 'Let me get the first knot tied. *Then* I'll work on the next.' It's just as true now as it ever was."

What Susan has just told me resonates in my brain, but I can't say why. *Let me get the first knot tied, then I'll work on the next.* It's an entire work ethic really, not just a pithy saying. And it sticks in my brain.

Talbot passes me another piece of boar.

"You know Gary as well as anyone," I say. "Do you think he really set those missiles to launch?"

Susan looks pained.

"I don't know, Ben. I've thought about that over and over since I watched him make that claim on television and I just can't say. Gary is a principled man and a decent person. However, if you're not in his circle, or don't share his beliefs, you're chaff. He's not hateful. And he's not vengeful. But he is self-righteous and judgmental."

"Enough to kill hundreds of thousands of people?"

"God, I hope not, Ben."

I finish the boar Susan gave me and look at the sun rising higher in the sky. By the time it's due to set late this afternoon, we'll all find out whether Gary Friedman is self-righteous enough to kill hundreds of thousands of people.

CHAPTER 40

I finish my chores and I get a call from Geness on my new blocked ID netacts. Thank you, Wilson. Only he and Gen know how to reach me.

"Hello," I answer. Gen is dressed in a black suit and sitting at her desk in the Oval Office.

"Hello, dear Ben," she says softly. "I'm missing you."

"Are you okay?" I ask. She looks fine. Tough. Determined.

"I'm tired, scared, and worried," she replies. "I've never been away from you this long before."

I am taken aback by her confession. Now *I* have to be tough and determined.

"You've done wonderfully, Gen. You've survived one hell of a week."

"Not knowing if you were alive was the worst," she says. Tears appear in the corners of her eyes. I can't watch that and not cry myself. I change the subject.

"Do you have any news on Gary?"

"I am so sorry," Geness says gazing at me. "I know you liked him."

I *still* like him. Gen goes on.

"The last word I had from his doctors was that he was comatose, but stable. They were still deciding what—if anything—they could do to relieve the swelling in his brain. He has significant damage in his right cerebrum. How exactly that will affect him if he survives won't be known until he regains consciousness."

"They're saying he might survive?"

"There is a chance," Gen clarifies, her tone cautious. "A small chance. If he does, he may not be able to talk or walk." Geness pauses to let me deal with that. Then she asks, "Have you seen Wilson this morning?"

"Only briefly. He's spending every second in his lab. He told me that he suspects Gary may have used a coding backdoor to access the missile programs. He still can't find evidence that Gary armed and set launch sequences like he claimed. Let's just hope Gary was just trying to intimidate Dung Tro."

"Mr. Tro is still prepping the Chinas for war," Geness responds. "If Friedman's communication chip winds up in their hands it will be a short war."

"But the security videos show that the assassin failed to retrieve it," I insist. "If Gary did remove the command chip from his body, he hid it after prepping the *Kennedy's* missiles. If he wasn't bluffing there won't be any war. And a lot fewer people will be speaking Mandarin in a few hours."

Gen shakes her head and goes quiet. In a moment she looks at me again. Her face troubled.

"What?" I ask.

Gen lifts an eyebrow.

"I didn't say anything."

"You will," I tell her, not unkindly. She can never hide it when something is on her mind.

"I've been approached by the permanent members of the Security Council to serve as president."

I instantly go numb.

"Carroll Lee conveyed the invitation to me early this morning," Gen continues.

My lips sort of move, but nothing comes out.

Gen frowns and stares at me.

"Ben? Are you alright?"

I get enough feeling back to nod.

"What about our life here?" I manage to murmur.

"You can have a dairy in New York, Ben. I promise."

"I don't want a dairy in New York," I say starting to get upset. "I have a dairy here that I like very much. Just needs a house. And you and Lodge."

"That's fine, too, honey," Gen says, consolingly. "I can go back and forth to New York."

"What?" I ask. "I'll be here and you'll be there?"

"Lodge and I will come to the farm as often as we can."

Now I feel dizzy. My wife and son will live somewhere else and I'll be here alone? The anger flows out of me and I crumple in despair. Some people face adversity with courage. Like Gary Friedman. Some with violence. Like Susan Talbot. I, apparently, respond with the blues.

"Ben?" Gen's voice pokes through my layers of self-pity.

"Sorry," I tell her. "I think I need some meds."

Gen purses her lips and frowns.

"That makes me sad, Ben."

TALL WAR

"It's just Valium."

Gen shakes her head.

"Benedict. Listen to me. Please. I promise that we'll make this work. Truly. I love you with all my heart."

My RediMedi must sense that I am teetering on the edge of despair. Without my even asking it patches me with an extra strong dose of Valium. Artificially calm, I look at Gen.

"If you love me so much, then tell me in person. I'm coming to the White House."

"Ben, I have to be in New York before Friedman's deadline this afternoon. General Wainwright and I have an emergency session with the Security Council to sort through strategies depending on what the orbiting missiles do or don't do. Believe me, Ben, I would do anything to stay and wait for you instead. But I can't."

"I'm coming anyway. If you're not there, I'll understand exactly what that means."

"Benedict, you're not being fair," Gen pleads.

"Don't care. I only care about you and me."

Geness just stares at me.

"Sorry, doll, I have to go," I tell her. "Gotta catch a train." With that I end the call. That was either the smartest or the dumbest thing I've ever done in my life. But off I walk to catch the ElecT to Washington to find out which one it was.

CHAPTER 41

I open the doors at the back entrance of the White House and head for the Oval Office in the West Wing. It is very quiet and barely lit. You'd think with a successful economy they'd put on a few lights. I walk down the hall where video replicas of the former presidents are hung. I recognize Washington and Lincoln, and Jeffrey Magnuson, the Final before Gen, but that's about it. No one minds them, for they are, in fact, dead, and their stories told. On the other hand, I am alive and working on not losing everything worth living for.

The door to the receptionist's office in front of the Oval Office is open. I can see Gen's desk. She is sitting at her desk, studying a monitor and occasionally using her keyboard. I walk up to the doorway to her office and wait for her to notice me. When she does, she runs to me, throws her arms around me, and gives me the best kiss I can remember. Then she puts her face against my neck and just holds me. When she looks at me again, she smiles.

"I am so happy to see you," she tells me and kisses me again. She takes my hand in hers.

"Me, too," I say lamely. "Seeing your face again was the only thing I could think about the whole time I was away from you."

"Come sit and talk to me," Gen says and leads me to one of the sofas in her office.

"Didn't we do it on this one?" I ask.

"Did indeed and will again," she says. "But not just now."

"No inclination?" I ask.

"Plenty of inclination," Geness assures me. "No time. I have to leave here in ten minutes to catch a plane to New York. We've got about six hours until we see if Friedman's missiles launch. Or if the Chinese attack. Either way, the folks at the United Nations have to cope with the final scenario."

"Did you accept the presidency of the Security Council?" I ask.

"Yes."

I look into Geness's eyes. They are troubled.

"Are you coming back?"

"Of course, Ben. You're here. Lodge is here."

"But we're not enough to keep you from going."

"Don't do this, Benedict. The world is facing its biggest crisis since Downsizing and if I can help save what everyone worked so hard to accomplish all these years, I must."

I shake my head.

"What? You really don't understand?"

"I understand. Doesn't make it hurt any less."

Gee. That makes me sound like a big baby. Gen reaches over and pulls my head against her breasts. She smells nice. Presidential nice, not I'm-wet-for-you nice. I better get used to that.

Gen suddenly tenses. I lift my head and both of us stare at Rigging Nash standing in the doorway to the Oval Office. Gen stands. I stand up next to her.

"Congratulations, Mr. Katz," Rigging sneers and walks in. "From what I've heard you've gone native—hiking, fishing, and hunting—all in the company of your *other* paramour."

"Fuck you, Rigging," my beautiful Geness tells him. "Why are you here, traitor?"

"Traitor?" Rigging almost chokes. "I am not the one who opened Earth's portals to the Martians," he says, his eyes narrow and mean. "That distinction belongs to you, Madam President."

"I opened doors, Mr. Rigging, but you and the other Benedict Arnolds you keep for company murdered without conscience. Throwing us into conflict with our own kind. Humans from Mars who reached out to us in peace."

"If you call trespassing on American soil and circling the globe with a spaceship full of missiles reaching out."

Gen grimaces.

"How did Dung Tro get to you, Rigging?"

"Au contraire, Gen," Rigging snaps and shakes his head. "I was the one who initiated conversations with the president of the Security Council and argued for preemptive action against the Martian Originals."

"I am truly sorry he ever listened to you," Gen says. "First, he got a dead spaceman. Now he's going to get a million dead Chinese."

Nash ignores her comment.

"You should point the accusing finger at your own spouse if you want to finger a heartless murderer."

I move toward Nash and yell, "Shut-up!"

He just looks at me and smiles.

"Why don't you tell your self-righteous wife that you and your space girlfriend tortured and murdered Adrian Modigliarty and four more agents the UN assigned to find you?"

Gen frowns and looks at me.

"That's just bullshit," I tell Nash. "Modigliarty and those so-called agents triggered the bombs on the space capsule on your orders trying to kill everyone on board." Nash looks offended. "I saw your two bodyguards on the spacecraft just before it blew, Rigging, and I overheard Adrian talking on his netacts to you."

Rigging Nash flushes and reaches inside his suitcoat breast pocket. In an instant, I know he came here to kill Gen. I launch myself at him and ram my head into his chest. He cries out, then he falls, gasping for breath. I put my knee on his throat and reach into his suitcoat myself. I pull out what looks like a miniature .44 Magnum. I don't know who illegally manufactured that, but I know a .44 when I see one, even a baby one. I've seen every single Dirty Harry movie. I aim the handgun at Nash then rise and step away. Gen grabs my arm and stares as Nash struggles for air.

"Call security," I tell her.

"There is no security!" she responds.

"Then call General Wainwright."

Geness is on the line instantly, and back off almost as fast.

"Wainwright says he'll have soldiers here in ten minutes. He said to incapacitate Nash and disable his weapon."

All right, I think. I look down at the man who came to murder my wife. I lower the barrel of the .44 and shoot Nash in the thigh. Gen screams. Nash screams. He's shot all right, but there's not a lot of blood, making it likely that he'll last until

Wainwright's men get here. Geness calls the general back and tells his aide to send medics along.

I decide I'm keeping the .44. There are other Rigging Nashs in this new world.

"You go," I tell Geness. "I'll wait for the soldiers. Just promise me that you really will come back to me."

Geness kisses me hard and flicks a little tongue at the end.

"Get the message?" she asks and walks toward the door.

"Indeed," I say and wave as she looks back. "It went straight to my pants."

"As it was meant to!" Gen exclaims and is out the door.

CHAPTER 42

I take an ElecT train back to the farm and milk the cows early. When four thirty comes and Gary's countdown concludes, I want to be watching a live vid feed, not scrubbing off cow teats. I finish and Susan and I both head for Gen's parents' home. We expect to see a tale of three cities gone forever unless Wilson actually managed to block Gary Friedman's Armageddon countdown.

Corkabee lets us in and starts to make coffee.

"Let me help," Susan volunteers. She gathers up fresh cups and saucers and moves the Final table on top of the Original kitchen table so we can all watch the world's future on the wall TV. I look at the clock on Corky's stove: 3:47. Part of me wishes I could just go back to the barn and milk my way through this mess. But the reality is I want to stare at the bad news just like everyone else on the planet. Corky works on the coffee, making sure there is enough for Susan to have a cup full.

I wonder if Wilson appreciates Corkabee? She loves him and she takes care of him. She's always there whenever he comes out of his lair to see his shadow. Oh, my. Six more hours of work. Gen used to be around like that for me. The first years of our marriage we were inseparable except for when I went to the barn to do my chores. I milked. She blogged. And we spent a lot of time in the sack. Then came Lodge. Then came the White House. And then came the Martians. Now she's gone and I'm on my own. Mooching off my in-laws. Whoever would have thought that tying the knot would have led to this?

Some tumbler clicks inside my brain and I realize with absolute certainty that I know where to find the hidden software backdoor that Gary Friedman used.

I jump up and catch Cork as she is pouring coffee.

"I need to see Wilson!" I say way too loudly.

"You know where he is," she says. "Remind him that he'll have to come to the kitchen if he wants to see what happens at four thirty. He refuses to have a television in his lab."

"Will do," I reply, already on my way out of the kitchen. The clock says it's 4:06. I head for Wilson's work place. He's glued to a monitor, but turns to look at me when I say hello.

"Hi," he replies, polite even in the face of certain doom.

"I know where you can find Gary's backdoor," I gasp.

"You do?" Wilson says matter-of-fact, not instantly swept away by my outsized claim.

"Talbot said something today that I think is the key," I tell him. "She said, 'Let me get the first knot tied. Then I'll work on the next.'" Wilson watches me without reacting. "Everyone says it on Mars," I add.

Wilson doesn't speak or move. It's obvious that he doesn't see the connection to Gary's backdoor.

TALL WAR

"If you pull up the master program that controls the missiles," I tell him, "and search each of its files to the end, one of them will have an option to go further. That option is Gary's backdoor."

"That's a lot of files, Ben," Wilson sighs. "But I think there is merit to your deduction and I can at least check the most obvious ones."

"Thank you, Wilson," I say relieved. He nods and turns to a new monitor. He wiggles his way into the orbiting ship's computers and in moments his screen is filled with file icons. Wilson scrutinizes them, then chooses one and opens it. He races through its contents only to close it and open another. Minutes seem to rush by as he opens file after file, scanning each one, then moving on to the next. Then he stops and searches one file very carefully. He glances at his watch. I look at mine. It is 4:21.

"Ben," he whispers, "I think you were right. The last window in this file contained blanks requesting a user ID and a password. I put in Gary's old ones and a new window opened to reveal all the *Kennedy's* actual software files, including the ones dedicated to managing the spaceship's missiles. What I accessed before was a brilliant *proxy* set, fooling me into thinking that I had gained access to the control software when all I really had was a dummy set of programs." Wilson shakes his head with admiration. "Woo, boy," he says, clearly impressed.

"Wilson," I cry. "It's 4:23!" Before he can react, Corkabee appears in the doorway and calls us.

"Wilson! Ben!"

Wilson doesn't respond. He has plunged into the newly revealed weapon files searching for the orbiting vessel's bona fide missile commands and controls.

I holler back to Cork.

"He's in Gary's backdoor!"

Cork runs over, her eyes huge.

"Go back and watch the TV," I encourage her. "In a few minutes everyone will know *everything* there is to know about how Wilson does here."

Corky runs for the kitchen. I look at Wilson. He is scrolling through options, picking rapidly, popping up window after window. I look at my watch: 4:25. Is that correct? I frantically look around for a clock. There's one on a distant wall: 4:26. Is there enough time for Wilson to get Gary's three active missiles reprogramed? I watch his every keystroke, ticking off every second. At exactly 4:30 Wilson lifts his forefinger and strikes the enter key.

He looks at me. His face is ashen. In moments Corkabee is at the door again.

"You better come," she says grimly.

Wilson gets down off his stool. I follow him. Talbot lifts both of us onto the big table and we sit on kitchen table chairs watching the television reporter on the wallscreen. He says that Gary Friedman's deadline for Dung Tro's surrender has passed. Not only is Tro still free, the Three Chinas have ratcheted their DefCon status to red. War seems inescapable no matter how Gary's threat plays out.

The announcer shares in a tense voice that the missiles—if actually fired—will take several minutes to enter the Earth's atmosphere and only then will they show up on tracking screens. I am dying to ask Wilson what he did in the last few minutes, but I keep my mouth shut and watch the television. Talbot stands, silently watching. Corky fidgets in her chair. Wilson just sits and

TALL WAR

stares at the TV, the only person here, or anywhere, who has any idea of what's going to happen next.

The screen switches to a view of the night sky over Beijing. The reporter cries out that he can see a missile. We gasp when we see it. A white streak plunging towards the Earth. The reporter shouts that two more missiles have been reported descending on Hong Kong and Shanghai. Then he loses it. He screams that the missile over Beijing will hit in ten seconds. "Ten! Nine! Eight!" he shouts. "Seven! Six! Five! Four! Three! Two!"

I close my eyes.

"One!"

CHAPTER 43

"What happened?" I cry.

"Ben!" Corky barks at me. "Open your goddamn eyes. Nothing happened!"

I open my eyes. The wallscreen is triple-split to show all three missile impacts. Massive clouds of dirt and debris whirl furiously. The missiles crashed to Earth, but their neutron bombs did not explode.

"Wilson!" I holler. He turns his head and looks at me. "You did it!"

He nods. And allows himself a small smile.

"Believe it or not," he says, "separate keystrokes were required to abort each missile launch. Yet only a single one was necessary to void the nuclear reactions and neutralize the neutron bombs. Thus, I had time to disarm the warheads, but I couldn't prevent the missiles from launching."

"Wilson, you saved the lives of a lot of people just now," Susan tells him. "You did the unbelievable." She looks at him

TALL WAR

with admiration. He smiles a goofy smile. I figure not too many six-foot blondes ever complimented him before.

Wilson looks at me.

"The fact is I couldn't have done it without you, Ben," he says. He explains to Talbot and Corkabee how Susan's Martian idiom inspired me to crack the location of Gary's hidden backdoor.

Susan smiles at me.

Corky can't resist a comment.

"Way to go, Ben," she says and smiles. "That's quite a brain you've been hiding all these years."

I blink.

Everyone laughs, including me. Man, what a relief to be laughing instead of crying. This is really the first happy thing that has happened to me in a week.

"There was an entire bank of dummy programs built as a subterfuge inside the spaceship's computer," Wilson says, happy to explain everything now. "I can't even imagine how many terabytes of memory that feat required in the twenty-second century. Fooled me good. I thought I'd voided Gary's commands earlier, but I had not. It was only Ben's cleverness that redeemed an old nerd-it-all like me. And I have to say, Friedman was able to access everything without anyone knowing. His backdoor was the true access to the missiles. The whole chip charade was a red herring to protect Gary's exclusive access to them."

Susan leans down and gives me a peck on the cheek.

"You're a brilliant guy," she tells me sweetly.

"Wilson," Corky says. "Call Gen immediately and explain what happened."

"Yes," Wilson says and has Geness up on the wallscreen in moments. Wherever she's at, I can see a huge UN emblem behind her. The tombstone of my marriage. The wallscreen's webcam captures all of us and displays exactly how Gen is viewing us in a corner display on our screen.

"You did it, Dad!" Gen bubbles, thrilled.

"It wasn't just me," Wilson demurs. "Ben was the one who found Admiral Friedman's secret backdoor. Only because of him was I able to disarm the nukes. I'm just sorry I didn't have enough time to stop the missiles from launching."

"Dad, what you did was great," Gen tells him. She looks at me. "And thank you, Ben. You have always been my hero."

I blush. Corky and Susan start hooting, which makes my ears catch on fire.

"I suggest you convene the Security Council as soon as you can," Wilson advises Geness. "The Chinese need to understand that their cities were spared only because of a technical intervention by the United States. There are twenty-one missiles remaining on board the Martian ship, and the United States considers them under United Nations control. Perhaps they'll be willing to consider surrendering Dung Tro in return for a UN guarantee that none of the missiles will be used against them." Wilson coughs self-consciously. "These are just suggestions, Gen," he demurs. "I'm no politician."

"Well, I think it sounds like a fair plan," Geness replies. "But the fact is that the ship and the missiles belong to the planet Mars, and as its representative, Lieutenant Commander Talbot, I would appreciate your thoughts on all of this."

"Given Admiral Friedman's incapacitation," Susan responds, "and may I add, his inappropriate use of our ship's missiles, I surrender the vessel and its armaments to you personally, Madam President. Do as you see fit."

We all watch Gen take that in. She rises magnificently to the occasion.

"It is an honor to have you on this planet, Officer Talbot," Geness responds. "I accept the vessel, but only until such time as circumstances allow for its return to you and the people of Mars."

"Thank you, Madam President," Susan says.

"Wilson, is it possible that Spaceman Talbot could work with you to prepare the ship's communications system for a transmission to Mars? I think it's time that the Mission Control authorities there learned from the *Kennedy's* communications officer that contact with Earth's governing authorities has been established and that a commitment had been extended to work with Mars to form a partnership *and* a friendship worthy of the great peoples of both planets."

Susan salutes Gen and beams.

"Hear, hear," Wilson says and Corky echoes it.

"Amen," Gen adds on her own. She and everyone else looks at me.

"Shit howdy!" I cry.

EPILOGUE

Excerpts from Benedict Katz's Thinking Cap

It's been a year since the Martian space capsule splashed down in the Potomac River. I have to say that nothing in my life has ever been the same after that. Some things got better. Some things got worse. The jury's still out on a whole lot of others.

The Earth has two governments now, split between East and West. The United Nations kept Europe, the Arab countries, the American nations, and the Central and South American states. All of Asia, Africa, and most of the Oceanic nations formed a new political entity. The Association of Asian-African Nations, ASSOAANS. Or as Corky calls it, the ASSONINES. Dung Tro is the chairman of the ASSOAANS.

My wife, Geness Jones, is the current president of the UN Security Council and lives in New York City with our son Lodge who is almost three. He and his mother come and visit me about one weekend in three.

Wilson is a world hero. With the joint agreement of the Martian government—represented by its newly appointed ambassador to the United Nations, Susan Talbot—the UN, and the ASSOAANS, he launched the remaining twenty-one neutron-tipped missiles from the MSS *John F. Kennedy* into the Pacific Ocean and sent the vessel back to Mars. I have to say that I, for one, am glad they're not flying around and around over my head any more.

Gary Friedman is recuperating well at Walter Reed Hospital in Washington, DC. He regained consciousness several weeks after the missile crisis ended, but the brain damage he sustained from the bullet wound deprived him of both his long-term memory *and* his ability to remember anything new for more than a few minutes.

Despite those setbacks Gary appears to be happy. Not only because the authorities on Mars have promised him an eventual brain transplant (an offer which he never remembers), but more particularly because Susan Talbot has moved in with him. Every day she has to reintroduce herself to Gary. But by all the reports I've gotten, he is still pretty darn good in the rack. Which reminds me, Gary's doctors found his dummy command chip the day he asked them why he had three testicles.

So, Wiki lovers—vultures and revisionists all—that's just about all I have to share about the return of the Originals and the way they impacted my life. You may ask how I feel about all the ups and downs, the crazy adventures, and how all the issues got resolved? My only regret is that I have been reduced to being a part-time husband and a mostly absentee father. Remaining rewarding, however, is the one thing that I count on and enjoy day after day. I am a full-time Virginia dairyman. Blessed to be working in America the beautiful, *and* happy with my living, my farm, and most of all, with my cows. *Mrrrr.*

The End

ACKNOWLEDGMENTS

I want to thank the true heroes of *Tall War*.
Vincent Chong, yet again, for his cover design and art;
Mark Meyer for copy editing at Professional Book Proofreading;
WZW for print formatting;
and Lionel Blanchard, the publisher who pioneered everything.

www.ingramcontent.com/pod-product-compliance
Lightning Source LLC
LaVergne TN
LVHW012250070526
838201LV00107B/312/J